ALSO BY JOHN ROLFE GARDINER

In the Heart of the Whole World

Great Dream from Heaven

Unknown Soldiers

Going On Like This

THE INCUBATOR
BALLROOM

THE INCUBATOR BALLROOM

A NOVELLA AND FOUR STORIES

John Rolfe Gardiner

ALFRED A. KNOPF   NEW YORK   1991

THIS IS A BORZOI BOOK
PUBLISHED BY ALFRED A. KNOPF, INC.

Published in the United States by Alfred A. Knopf, Inc., New York, and
simultaneously in Canada by Random House of Canada Limited,
Toronto. Distributed by Random House, Inc., New York.

Some of the stories in this work were originally published in:
The New Yorker: "In Dairyland," "Karaghala's Daughter," "Our Janice,"
"World After Dark," and "Game Farm" (chapter 1 of the novella "The
Incubator Ballroom"). *New Virginia Review*: "Starblanket" (chapter 4 of the
novella "The Incubator Ballroom").

Library of Congress Cataloging-in-Publication Data

Gardiner, John Rolfe.
The incubator ballroom : a novella and four stories / John Rolfe
Gardiner.—1st ed.
p. cm.
ISBN 0-679-40033-8
I. title
PS3557.A7113I54   1991
813'.54—dc20   90-43242
CIP

Manufactured in the United States of America

FIRST EDITION

to Berry Morgan

There's many a strong farmer
Whose heart would break in two,
If he could see the townland
That we are riding to;
Boughs have their fruit and blossom
At all times of the year;
Rivers are running over
With red beer and brown beer . . .

—W. B. Yeats
"The Happy Townland"

CONTENTS

THE INCUBATOR
BALLROOM

1. GAME FARM

When Michael's mother said her three nieces could have been hotel girls, she didn't mean anything cheap. Quite the opposite. In Roanoke there was a set of families who shunned the outlying country clubs and made do with the city's grand old hotel. Their coming out parties were held there. Their early dating and finest evenings were in its elegant dining room, among the marble columns of its panelled reception hall, and in its underground cocktail bar.

Michael's mother and his Aunt Ailene had been presented at the hotel in the same season. When their weddings came— Ailene's nine years before Michael's mother's—the receptions had been held in the same familiar room. But long before his mother married, she had lost her brother Eddie to a small farm in a forsaken, northern corner of the state. And one reason Eddie had given for removing himself and Ailene to that wilderness was precisely to escape the society that still circled the old hotel—a society in which his sister had been an eligible beauty for too long.

A renunciation. She took it hard that her brother should attack her just for taking her time, waiting for the right man, and using the hotel's elegant cover—its salon, bar, and ball-room. Still, they kept in touch. As Michael later came to understand it, his mother could forgive Eddie's boorish reclu-sion if he could forgive her long dalliance. When she married a cotton salesman from South Carolina, the dalliance became moot, but Eddie continued selfishly secluding his wife and daughters, who were losing tone on the banks of a northern river.

Michael's mother had visited often, perhaps with a rescue in mind. She had seen for herself. Flies and mosquitoes with free flight over an unscreened porch. Dark water and detritus in the ice trays. Ailene fighting for the girls' grammar against the influence of a hired man and his son. Unsuitable clothes. Long hippie skirts on the children when they were playing in the fields, and jeans when they should have been in something nice for the evening.

Her brother had something to prove. He shaved his head, and wore black pajamas in the fields. According to her, he came ignorant to corn and machinery, thinking high intelli-gence could get him through. Actually, at the mercy of swinging-door help, though some coincidence of weather and the grain markets had brought him an early profit.

Uncle Eddie, according to Michael's mother, had been an easy, irreverent scholar. The Latin prize in his high school. At the university, classics, in which, she said, he was doing beau-tifully when he dumped them for psychology. As if he could have sustained interest long enough to become a head-doctor. Eddie, she maintained, could never settle. A wonder he'd got-ten Ailene, a hotel girl, to marry and accept the upcountry horrors.

With her censure she was creating the legend of a family pioneer. A forecast of a bad end for brains in a barnyard was her modest way of saying, "My brother could have been anything. Never mind that he's chosen to go nowhere and be nothing." If she hadn't respected him, why so many visits to the farm before she was married? And afterward, why had she so often left her only child, Michael, to the care of Eddie and his family?

Years later, Michael could still remember the exciting news: "Can you believe it? Eddie's turned the place on the Potomac into a game farm." Even more exciting, Michael's mother and father, needing private time again for the long quarrel their marriage had become, were sending him up for the summer. Eight years old, he was being passed along to Eddie and Aunt Ailene. And to his three older cousins, Georgia, Annalee, and Grace. Wild girls of the north, in his mother's estimation—the ones he couldn't wait to see.

Michael knew he shouldn't have shown such delight to his parents. But everything was turning out perfectly. At Easter he had seen the redbuds and dogwoods making little chapels of color in the dark woods. And his teacher had squeezed his arm gently and promised to promote him to the third grade.

Then the odd and wonderful report that his uncle's farm—the house, the woods behind, the sloping meadow down to the wide bottomland—had been turned over to the pleasure of a game. He wondered if his cousins would teach him Monopoly. Awkward to learn on arrival that there were no plans for checkers in the parlor or badminton in the fields; that his uncle was raising ducks for hunters.

That summer Michael had been put on the bus in Roanoke and sent up the valley in a jacket and tie to Winchester.

The whole Mason family came to collect him at the depot. He sat in the very back of their station wagon, and the girls kept turning in their seat to fuss over him and protest against the inches he'd grown during the winter.

The sisters had always been eager for his visits. He'd been told that when he was a toddler, the big one, Georgia, had pushed him up and down the long cinder drive in a carriage. For a season he was her doll. She showed him off to anyone who would listen to outrageous matronly chatter. "A hard labor with this one. I don't really know if I want another." She was twelve then, quite theatrical, with corkscrew curls, pretty red springs that seemed to connect her bouncy head to her shoulders.

Georgia had changed. She looked at Michael as if a judgment had been made about him, not entirely favorable, and her full attention was going to be impossible. Michael noticed that her nose had gotten larger, and she was saying "unbearable" about each thing that displeased her.

The second sister, Annalee, was tugging on his silly tie, holding his gaze while she made fun of his grown-man outfit. Annalee was plump, alert for fun, with green eyes that she already knew how to promote with a green scarf. "If you get scared in the attic," Annalee told him, "you can sleep in my room." She talked about a blacksnake skin in the attic until Aunt Ailene told her to be quiet.

The youngest, Grace, silent up to then, asked him suddenly in a remarkable, deep voice, "Do you know how old I am?" He was startled, as if quizzed by a bullfrog with spider legs. He didn't care to guess, unaware that the challenge in her little, whiskey throat was only the armor of the smallest, and that the proud answer—"ten years old"—was scorned by sisters already thirteen and eighteen. Grace reached back to tousle his hair as Annalee had done a moment before.

"Leave Michael alone," Aunt Ailene told them, and she said to Uncle Eddie, "How could his mother send him all that way by himself?"

He remembered the shadow falling over him at those words, and he remembered crying inconsolably in the back of the Masons' car. And how, when they got to the farm, Annalee had taken him for a tour to cheer him. "We haven't stopped growing corn," she said, "we've just added ducks."

The duck hatchery was the old barn, and a smooth concrete floor had been poured and rough boards nailed up for interior walls. On one side, where the floor was covered with sawdust, hundreds of baby ducks crowded under steel hovers, keeping warm. Across the room a great wooden cabinet hummed like a refrigerator. "It's not cold in there," Annalee told him. Inside, a large drum filled with eggs in wire baskets turned almost as slowly as the hand of a clock.

"I'm forbidden to do this," Annalee said, opening a panel and reaching in for an egg. She moved to a row of switches and suddenly the only light in the barn was coming from a little hole next to her. She held the egg up to the beam, showing him a small, dark place inside. "That's blood," Annalee said, "little rivers of blood."

"Annalee! Are you in there?"

The lights came on and her father was standing across the floor. She was sent to the house and Michael's tour of the hatchery was completed by Uncle Eddie, who took him into the penned areas with wire partitions where hundreds of mallards were separated according to age. The oldest, his uncle explained, were down on the river waiting for the dinner bell. This was going to be Michael's daily chore, ringing the big iron bell each evening, watching the ducks fly home over the trees to the protein pellets waiting for them in their wire shelters.

When the hunters came that summer, Michael was forbidden to go outside. From his attic window he would hear his uncle's voice calling from the release ramp beside the pens, and moments later, the answering reports of shotguns from the meadow below the woods.

Alone, there was time to consider the mysteries of the farm: why Uncle Eddie's black pajamas went into a separate hamper, and why he did his own laundry; why, each morning, Aunt Ailene made her girls drink a measured cup of grapefruit juice; why the surviving ducks flew home in the evenings only to be shot at another day.

Big cousin Georgia was locking her door for hours at a time. When she considered Michael she was apt to speak about him, not to him. About the "unbearable situation" in Michael's home in Roanoke. "Never mind her," Aunt Ailene said. "She's going down to the university in September. She has reading to do. She's worried about her skin."

Annalee became his summer friend, treating his homesickness with hand-in-hand trips to a creek in the woods. Together they took off their clothes and waded into the water. Before he went home to Roanoke, Annalee gave him stationery with envelopes addressed to her.

His mother came for him at the end of August and was freshly appalled by conditions and her cold greeting by the girls. "What did you do all summer?" she asked him.

"I went swimming."

Alarmed, she recalled that she'd never packed his bathing suit.

At home Michael thought of Annalee standing next to

him in the creek, and could not write, too ashamed of his handwriting and the meagerness of the news he was able to spell. He supposed he'd see her the next year. But his mother wouldn't talk about another trip. She didn't like what was happening to his cousins. Something had come over them—of all things, an upcountry snobbery. "The Masons have had enough of you for a while," she said.

The next spring, when Aunt Ailene wrote to ask which week he'd be coming, his mother was adamant. She took him visiting with her to friends in Lynchburg and Staunton. He remembered his humiliation in both cities, being made to stand and recite three verses from Hiawatha. Very much on display, the only prize of her marriage.

Michael's mother kept the memory of his cousins alive with lament and denunciation. "Coming to no good," she assured him. He wished he could be with them on their way to this bad end. There were brief visits to the Potomac farm, each one unsatisfactory. Years passing, but never without reference to his cousins. "That was the year Georgia matured so suddenly," or "That was the year Annalee wasn't pretty."

Michael was fourteen before the Masons were allowed to have him for another season. He was still anxious to go, though there was summer sport ahead of him in his own city. And a door to watch on his block where a young lady went in and out.

Aunt Ailene had almost begged for him. They needed a steady young man, was the way she put it. Someone to give Eddie and the girls a hand, since the last help had run off. And something to reestablish her connection with Roanoke.

On no condition, Michael's mother said, could he be allowed to handle a gun. With that solemn contract he was allowed up the valley again on the Greyhound. He travelled with the old memory of Annalee beside him in the water, wondering if there would be more secret swimming.

His aunt and Grace delighted in his enormous changes. So tall! And the wonderful, naughty hair, as long as their own. His uncle seemed pleased to see him. Not Annalee. She was polite, distant, betraying him as Georgia had before her, pre-occupied with things that couldn't be shared by a young-boy cousin. He arrived in short sleeves, biceps for Annalee, but it was lithe Grace who ran her hands down his arms and gave him the big hug. Passed down again by the sisters, like old clothes.

"Georgia isn't even here," Grace said, when they were all in the car driving home. She had the same deep voice that cracked when she hurried it.

"Georgia is taking work in Charlottesville for the summer," Aunt Ailene said quickly.

"A little Roanoke camouflage," Uncle Eddie said.

"Be quiet," Aunt Ailene told him. "What do you know about Roanoke society? You never entered it."

Uncle Eddie turned around at the wheel and announced to everyone, "You don't enter society. You're born into it."

Grace leaned over to whisper in Michael's ear, "Georgia's living with her boyfriend from college, and she hasn't even had her party yet."

Sixteen, Grace was a power on the farm, giving crisp orders, even to Annalee. The hatchery was in full production. Ducks were being sold to other farms and wholesalers. Grace could run the whole thing herself, she told Michael, pleased to think she was in charge of eight thousand eggs. Michael watched attentively as she hurried from task to task, sweating through her T-shirts, cursing incompetence.

"We have to teach them to fly," she said like a goddess. He didn't believe it. Then he and Grace spent hours forcing one young mallard after another up a ramp from which he could either plop to earth or spread his wings and glide. In time each bird raced its wings, gained altitude through an opening in the trees, and flew down over meadow and corn-fields to the river.

That summer, while the gunmen waited, ready in their meadow blinds, Michael worked the release gate with Grace, who called encouragement to the ducks as they took off. "Fly high, beauties!" She said the drakes' white neck-rings were their charms against buckshot.

Obedient, Michael allowed her to take his arm and hurry him along from one job to the next. And from time to time, Uncle Eddie would show up, taking them by surprise. To see how they were treating the eggs. Or how they were treating each other.

Michael had been staying in the attic again. Old enough now to think of the house as a network of exciting bedrooms, he was directly above Georgia's empty chamber, which she did not want used or explored in her absence. Next to that was the master bedroom, from which Michael could hear the muffled voices of his aunt and uncle in the dark. At the end of the hall, from a room shut tight, Annalee's tape machine played provocative music not quite low enough to be secret.

Grace was downstairs in a tiny room off the kitchen—quarters that had been used by the maid of a previous household. After the family turned their lights out, there was no telling what Grace might be doing. Through the attic window Michael sometimes saw her in the moonlight, moving around the duck pens, checking her flock, or walking toward the river, stargazing.

Aunt Ailene kept the door to her room open at night. If Michael came downstairs to use the bathroom, she would call, "Is that you, Michael?" or "Is that you, Annalee?" Sometimes she called all their names, "Annalee? Michael? Grace?"

In the house one afternoon, seeking relief from Grace's energy and orders, Michael stole a beer from the refrigerator and was gulping it quickly in the side room Uncle Eddie used for his library. A small gilt-edged volume on the shelf caught his eye. Catullus? It was inscribed to Edward Mason II, first in Latin. Under that, in ink now pale blue, a line his uncle must have written to himself: "At last the poetry gets dirty."

Skipping through the pages, as if he could translate and find out if it was true, he heard his uncle's voice behind him. "If you're going to drink beer, pour it in a mug." More concerned with the effect of the book, which he took from Michael's hand. Replacing it on the shelf, he said, "Not worth a glance. Grace is looking for you."

Uncle Eddie moved to a window from which he could see Grace in the duck pens. His forehead against a pane, he began to speak in a peculiar voice. "If you're a stranger, anything is possible, even romance, but hospitality is difficult." Almost mumbling, he said, "If you're family, you're welcome in the bosom forever."

Meditation or lecture? Michael couldn't say which.

"Where are you, Eddie?" Aunt Ailene was coming through the door. "What are you telling Michael? What is his mother going to think?"

Michael left them arguing about whether he should be allowed to drink beer, and what his mother would think about that. And for the rest of the afternoon he moved eggs for

Grace, even obeyed when she told him to explain what was going on in Roanoke.

He exaggerated. There had been shouting as far back as he could remember. His father had inherited part of a small railroad with mortgaged equipment, and this complicated a pending divorce. Lawyers were taking years deciding how to divide things, how to divide him.

His parents still occupied the same house, living in separate rooms, each maintaining a squatter's right, lest a move jeopardize legal standing. Considered a split pair by their Roanoke crowd, who danced and played cards together, they were each "seeing new friends" as their circle put it. Even careful to balance infidelities.

"Your mother was a long time getting married, wasn't she?" Grace asked him. "I suppose if you waited that long you could expect to catch a layabout."

"He's a cotton rep," Michael corrected her.

"What's that?"

He could only tell her what he'd heard at home: "A man who spends too much time in other cities asking pansies to put more natural fibers in the clothes they design."

It seemed there was something wrong with what he'd told Grace earlier. "People can get divorced," she said, "and decide the other things later." Big news, late arriving. Why hadn't he known that? "Anyway, your mother was one of those hotel people, wasn't she?"

"So was yours," Michael snapped back.

"Yes, but she didn't use upstairs rooms."

Struck dumb, he'd never considered the guest rooms of the old hotel as anything more than the sad quarters of travellers. He watched a fertilized egg fall to the floor. His fault. Grace's head turned back to business.

After a while she said, "You know, you're getting to be almost as old as I am." A two-year gift he was pleased to accept as he watched her lashes flutter at the tips of her long, pale bangs.

Among the visiting hunters there was much talk about makes and values of shotguns, chokes, bores, shot patterns. Though Uncle Eddie had his own shotgun, it hung over the mantle in his study like a museum piece. He shied away from the he-man chitchat. On the side of the ducks, he was more interested in the hatching and nurturing.

Most of the hunters did not care to pluck and eat. They left the dead with Aunt Ailene with best wishes—gifts of the mighty. She accepted politely, as if there were room for another shot-ridden carcass in her freezer.

One weekend a party of huge, happy men arrived—members of a professional football team down from New Jersey, with shotguns on loan. They were pointing them at each other, taking mock aim, saying things like: "You're glad this isn't loaded."

They set off for the blinds, and before they reached the meadow one of the guns discharged. A hail of shot fell on the hatchery's metal roof. Uncle Eddie went down the hill after the men, tore up their check, and told them to get off the property. They came up the path shamefaced and silent. But back in their van, they spun their wheels all the way down the driveway.

As Michael watched, his uncle's anger passed quickly into meditation. "At first, the egg has no air cell," he said softly. "But the shell is porous, moisture escapes. What do we make of that?" Dreaming of an answer? Looking around and seeing that his nephew had been listening, he turned embarrassment into an order. "Make sure they're getting enough calcium. We don't want any more leakers."

"Georgia is too quiet," Aunt Ailene announced when the summer was half over. Annalee was sent down to visit and report back on her sister's "involvement." He was a lanky boy, they heard, with gentle manners. A black-haired swimmer doing laps in the university pool when Georgia had come upon him alone. As Annalee told it, her sister had been immediately wounded in love by the undulations of his long body at work on the butterfly stroke.

And what was happening this summer?

"Nothing much," came the report from Annalee, who had been introduced to another boy in Charlottesville, and had begun to negotiate with her parents for time of her own there.

Aunt Ailene's "absolutely not" was undercut by Uncle Eddie's indecision, and the visit dragged on. After a week of long-distance debate the girls stopped answering their phone.

"The two of them are useless anyway," Grace said. "So what's changed? Michael and I do all the work."

"So why is Michael still in the attic?" Uncle Eddie asked, and Aunt Ailene moved his things down to Annalee's room where he could feel "more like real family."

What he felt was one floor closer to Grace, who would lean against him on the way from house to barn, and ask, "Where would I be without you?"

With Annalee gone it was that much easier to work hard for Grace. Standing beside her at the incubator, shifting eggs to the hatching trays, he imitated the robot action of her long, thin arms, still trying to please her with labor.

One evening on the way up to the house she asked him, "What would we do if my parents weren't here?"

"I suppose we'd work just as hard," he said, hoping he'd guessed right.

That same evening his mother called from Roanoke because he hadn't written a single line. He kept telling her, "no, everything's fine," until Aunt Ailene took the phone away from him. And he heard her say, "They're darling together. He's devoted to her."

Grace disappeared, and Michael went up to bed, slowly counting the steps in the staircase, the way he did at home, reluctant to leave anyone awake behind him. Later, he was doing his other number trick, counting the deep breaths it takes to reach sleep, when his door opened, and Grace came to his bed. "This can only happen once," she said.

In the morning, right in front of her mother, Grace asked if he'd slept well, and if he was ready to make ducks walk the plank. Aunt Ailene was measuring out grapefruit juice, getting them off to another healthy day.

Grace was no sooner out the front door with him than she asked, "Was it nice for you?" moving too quickly for him, from deceit to pleasure. He couldn't tell her there had been nothing in his life to compare it to.

Something had gone wrong the night before. As soon as Grace had left his room she had not seemed beautiful anymore, but an ungainly farm girl who might need secrets and apologies. Lying in bed he had begun to compare her face unfavorably with Georgia's and Annalee's. Grateful for her pledge, "only once," he fell asleep. Now her knobby knees were sticking through holes in her jeans. With sunburned arms and neck she looked her usual part again—hired help living in maid's quarters—the way he was used to her.

"Don't worry," Grace said. They were hardly out of sight

of the house when she took his hand, raised it to her small breast, and told him, "I'm going to take care of you."

While they taught ducks to fly, Grace tried to convince him he was safe with her. "If cousins can't help each other into the world," she said, "who can?" They were pushing the mallards onto the ramp. Each time they put a duck on at the bottom, another at the top was forced, against its will, into the air. With this for sport, they bet on the birds: which would fly to the river, and which would have to try again.

At supper that night Uncle Eddie asked Michael if he knew why the lights in the barn were kept on all night, every night. Michael didn't know. "Because if ducks are startled in the dark, they stampede. Grace knows that. I'm surprised she hasn't told you."

Before the meal was over his uncle had another pointed question, more husbandry. "How do you tell their sex before they grow up?"

"Stop it, Eddie," Aunt Ailene said.

"By their voices," Uncle Eddie told him, leaning forward with the news. "The hens honk and the drakes belch."

Grace had left the table.

Later, awake in his bed, Michael was surprised at how quickly his plans changed. He rose, put on pants, and went barefoot from his room. In the hall he felt like a child playing Red Light, Green Light, the floor squeaking "Stop" at each small advance. It took him several minutes to reach the stairs. On the ground floor he went straight through the kitchen corridor to Grace.

"Why only once?" he asked.

A moment later, a light shone under the door, and Aunt Ailene called, "What's going on in there?"

Next morning, first thing, Aunt Ailene phoned his mother, who was starting north immediately. Grace could guess what his mother had said: "When I think they could have been hotel girls." Meaning Georgia, Annalee, and Grace. There was no counting the number of times his mother had said it, this refrain that gently mocked her own life.

"Never mind, young lady." Aunt Ailene was stripping all the beds, doing the white laundry with angry amounts of Clorox.

By the time his mother came, Georgia and Annalee were on their way too, answering their mother's call for help. They arrived, surprising Michael with raised, adult eyebrows. He understood his aunt was making the house respectable again, filling the rooms with legitimate company.

The older sisters with even tans and nicely made-up faces had become a team with their own agenda. It was clear they thought Grace would have to wait a long time for honest love.

As Michael packed he could hear his mother downstairs asking someone, "What can you expect in a house that doesn't even have a television?" She was moving through the ground-floor rooms, taking inventory of the house's deficiencies. And the next minute she was upstairs, standing arms akimbo in his doorway, telling Michael, "It's going to take a long time to live this down."

2. REAL FARMING

When Ailene left Eddie and went back to Roanoke, she told Grace, "Stay and be damned." Not so much a curse of the moment as a prediction of things to come. "He'll let you do anything, honey. Be careful."

Grace gave no thought to leaving with Ailene. Twenty-two by then, managing three hundred acres, she had already spoken at a Grange supper, where she was introduced as "the young lady who does it all." She had a cadre of young men who would work through the summers for her at very low wages. A self-replenishing pool of boys, some of them still in high school, who came to her for five dollars, and less, an hour, throwing hay bales and tanning their backs under her appreciative eye.

"Grace's help," they were called in the family, boys who were never going to be farmers themselves. With fathers who now called their own land "real estate" and had become experts with the county's zoning map. The young men came asking for summer work, willing labor. So obviously her admirers, her protectors. Grace knew that some of them came just to be close to her, that she excited them with her independence and command, and eyes that darkened when their flirtation became pointed. The farm was first in her life. She worked right alongside them, proving it. If some of them were waiting for a turn with her in a far field or under a fence, let them dream on.

Grace had never chosen any of them for special favors. "Are you being careful, dear?" Her mother's repeated question freighted with misplaced fear of heartache, defilement, infection, pregnancy. Fast in high school, slow on the farm? Ailene couldn't believe it. Grace thought it might be a relief to have Ailene in Roanoke where her curiosity could be handled at a convenient remove.

Grace, a local oddity. A heron standing on a cow's back, an ant pulling a huge wasp through the grass, a red fox trotting along the top of a stone fence, and Grace, against odds, eking profit from the family farm. Another feat of country magic. Proving wrong the extension agent who said it couldn't be done. There was no honest commodity farming left in the county. Alfalfa wouldn't pay out either.

Changing the place from her father's game farm to her own hay operation, Grace had been blessed by weather luck. She'd made three cuttings in each of her first two years, giving orders to the sky. "Don't you rain now!" or "Let it pour!" And the rains had come with a gracious timeliness. Holding off, giving the mown alfalfa time to cure, then coming on to push up a new crop.

Her young men had come to think that as a farmer, Grace was charmed. They did weather chants on the hay wagons. And the goddess they sang to in their mock prayers was Grace. She helped them all feel important, and not just as muscle. They were the spirits that kept the place a farm instead of real estate.

Another safe year? "I understand. Watch my pH. And get a spray for the other thing." Grace hung up the phone, and Ailene was suddenly beside her asking, "Are you sure you're going to the right man, dear?"

"Not a gynecologist. That was Southern States. They're coming to lime the lower fields."

It wasn't just Ailene who wondered where agriculture was leading Grace. Her sisters Annalee and Georgia called with dutiful regularity, checking up on farm life. Who would Grace's help be this year? How long did she expect to go on like this? Making her profit off the same kind of young people a fast-food franchise would hire. Grace had remarkable good cheer for her sisters. They were the ones who had made mouths for their mirrors, and run off to Charlottesville to find early husbands among the university boys. Leaving the hayfields to Grace. If they were happy in their marriages, why did they keep phoning home?

For Grace they had provided the news about Michael. In his first semester at the university he had gone beyond hippie, dirty and growing hair beyond belief, and leaving suddenly without taking exams. He'd still be all right for the farm, she thought, but by then, no address. Just California. In the first year of his transformation he had written Grace once to declare his spiritual growth, and though it was four years late, his apology for being silly on the farm. "Not for crossing the line with you, but for being so immature when I got to the other side."

Grace's mother announced her departure, but a month later her unpacked luggage was still spread around the master bedroom—a lingering threat. That month her father retreated into his study. He'd come out from time to time with a reproachful question, or sit where Grace could hear him ask himself, "Why, why?"

According to Ailene, he could have looked in almost any room of the house for the answer, including the bedroom. Instead he consulted his library, relating Ailene's planned escape to a line from his latest reading. "A bad environment increases the locomotion of all species." He told Grace to think of a tick chased by a lighted match, a man crawling out of a desert, and your mother after twenty-five years in the country. "Rather a slow reaction time."

He'd been the black pajama farmer, the grownup hippie to the natives along the river. "In black you perspire heavily," he'd told them. "The sweat evaporates. Evaporation is a cooling process. The Vietnamese figured it out long ago." Securing his eccentricity he'd raised mallards, introducing the game farm concept to the county.

The way her mother saw it, Eddie, after growing bored

with his ducks, had thrown the family land at Grace with an irresponsible challenge. "See what you can do with it," baiting her vanity with a test she wouldn't refuse. Immediately, Grace had set the surviving mallards free along the river. She brought her father a paper to sign from the bank, bought another tractor and the wagons, all in preparation for hay. Thoroughbred horse people were paying three and four dollars a bale.

Her father could admire his land again as she bucked the trend of specialty croppers—people in hydroponic lettuce, asparagus, shiitake mushrooms, shrubbery—the ten-acre wonders working their small visions on the subdivided landscape around her. She was paying no mind to her mother's warning: "You're one of his experiments."

In fact, Eddie was brooding, taking comfort only in his library. He dusted off his classics, took down the thin, prize volume of Catullus and chuckled over his naughty poems. And he tried to calm the family, assuring them that all Mason land was divided into three parts. Georgia and Annalee could relax. Eventually the farm would be split equally among his daughters.

For Grace the three parts were the sections she chose for alternate planting. Each year she would fertilize and reseed one-third of the farm, keeping her alfalfa thick and healthy, as it was then in late May for her young men and the first cutting. Seeing the fields were almost ready, they came to sign on for the summer, one and two at a time.

A new hand who called himself Tommer, long for Tom, seemed much too old and mature to Ailene to be accepting low wages. "He wears a shirt," she noticed. "That's nice. What does his father do?"

He had good shoulders and he owned the haybine they would cut with this year, but Ailene had to talk about his penetrating eyes. Grace thought Tommer would get along well with the Wilson brothers, Paul and Wesley, coming back for a third season.

With the Wilsons it was matching cases of back acne that bothered her mother. The way they roasted themselves under the summer sun. Not at all the right treatment in the long run. Grace refused to embarrass Paul and Wesley with the name of her mother's dermatologist. Sixteen and eighteen, the Wilsons were clever mimics of Grace's deep, cracking voice, her manly stride, entertaining the younger boys, the wagon tenders, with their imitations. All part of her crew's fascination with their lady farmer.

Last to arrive this year was Billy Johnson, who'd been in Future Farmers with Grace in high school. Should have been making something of himself by now according to Ailene, instead of wandering in his own neighborhood, just getting by.

This one, too, was known to Ailene by his bare upper body as it appeared in the fields next to Grace. There was a small diamond on his shoulder, pale blue and crooked, a homemade tattoo. Billy had asked for extra evening work to be doing things for Grace after the others were gone.

"He's harmless," she told her mother. "Just grazing."

This was Grace's truth. That in the evening when she climbed the stairway to solitary sleep, she would be thinking affectionately of whatever member of her crew had most pleased her that day. And lying down with a T-shirt for a nightgown and a hand between her legs, she teased and gratified the center of her longing. Only in this way was she sleeping through her payroll, bestowing favors on them all.

Ailene was working her way through the house, making a pile of everything that could be called hers, and more, paintings off the walls and silver from the sideboard. "I'm taking the Moran," she'd shouted down the bare stairway. Unprovoked, Eddie seldom moved from his den. "Damn you, who do you think you're going to get to make your meals?"

Was the answering noise from his room "Whom whom whom," or "Ommmmmmmm"? They couldn't be sure.

Ailene had actually packed and was living out of her suitcases. She was staying, she said, until Grace's help was fully organized for the season. She could not accept that two of the new boys had no references at all. And she kept finding other reasons for delay.

Georgia, in Roanoke, seeing a chance to be helpful, gathered up her sister Annalee, and the two of them drove up the valley to the farm without husbands for "family conferences."

"Look at you!" Annalee greeted Grace. "Healthy as sin, I suppose."

"Still doing nothing about your hair," Georgia said.

The three sisters standing before the pier glass in the front hall, making two Renoirs and a Giacometti in the mirror, Grace the rough skinny figure, her lips tight in this moment of mutual reappraisal which made her odd woman out.

In the way they turned to regard themselves in the glass Grace saw her sisters' satisfaction with the sensible direction their lives had taken, the way they did their full, pink faces, the ample way they filled their nicely tailored clothes. They were making their love for her plain with gifts—a blouse of Egyptian cotton, a silver bracelet, and the bright chatter of sisterhood.

But right away Grace saw other news in their collusive glances—planning afoot from which she'd been excluded. They weren't here to help outdoors; no brogans or jeans in their wardrobes.

"We're not taking sides," Annalee said. She had come home with a practical air, an agenda for give-and-take. "Of course he'll talk to you," she assured Ailene. Her up-front advice was to avoid blame. "If you get into fixing blame, there's no end to it."

Georgia was more cautious, and Grace thought the way she talked she might have been comforting the ill. "Mother, wouldn't you like to put your clothes back in the bureau?"

Nothing doing. Ailene's things remained packed for the sudden departure that could no longer be sudden. On this, the first evening of their reunion, they were able to get Eddie to the dinner table. He came quite amiably out of his room, then gently scolded Georgia and Annalee for the racket they'd been making in the house since their arrival. "As if the walls have to know everybody's business."

Ailene said nobody knew his business, which got Annalee started again. "Anger is no good here. You both have to try introspection." And her mother finally said what Grace had been thinking. "All this trendy advice of yours, Annalee. It sounds secondhand. Are you having trouble at home?"

Grace was grateful her sisters had returned. Perhaps they could heal the family while she ran the farm. Outside most of the time, Grace could only guess what was being said in the house. She ate breakfast before the others, came back to grab a bite and refill the ice-water jugs at noon, and was in the fields again until early evening dew made the hay too damp to bale. The only chore her sisters had taken on was preparation of the evening meals.

"What are you really up to here?" Annalee had asked her, as if there must be a liaison that Grace would be ashamed to admit to, something illicit going on within the demimonde of her hired hands.

"I'm making a real farm," she said. "No land bank. No government scam." There were things she shouldn't have to explain. Morning light on the new green-and-yellow machines. Their rhythm and counter-rhythm over the hills, the rake rattling off a windrow for the baler thumping its mechanical appetite in another field. And the soft guttural of tractors in the distance, showing their pipes first as they came over the rises. Engines that could excite you with their superfluous power.

Annalee and Georgia were ignoring the beautiful gray-green carpet of alfalfa Grace had spread before them. As they watched the farm's progress from the porch, their eyes were on her and the way she moved among her help. Baby sister Grace, her little breasts scarcely hidden under her threadbare, sleeveless blouse, balancing on the lurching wagon after a terrible sweat in the mow, going back to the fields, mixing her musk with the musk of the men.

Georgia and Annalee up at the house all day, stirring the emotional stew their mother was in, could only wait until evening to tell Grace to shower and make herself decent, unappreciative of the small miracle she'd accomplished. Another day of real farming for her men. A crew that deserved to fall in the grass and guzzle the beer she'd brought them when the work was done.

"Eddie," her mother said, "these aren't wicked sisters. Grace isn't Cinderella. You don't know the effect she has on those boys."

The family had noticed a light from the hayloft that sometimes went on and off after dark as if blinking a message to the house—Billy Johnson, who had been staying overnight in the barn, signalling goodnight to Grace. Her father knew about it. Why should she explain this innocent thing to sisters perpetually dressed as if fancied extramarital lovers might pop on the scene?

After their first week on the farm Eddie told them at table, "Go back to Roanoke and tend to your own husbands."

Grace saw that her father would only speak to them at meal time, and evasively. "Why won't you make an effort?" Annalee asked him.

"A farmer's heart runs on organic batteries," he'd said.

"But you're not a farmer," Georgia crossed him. She was determined to stay on until this thing was settled, and Annalee, not to be outdone in family duty, wouldn't leave before Georgia. Instead of discouraging their mother, they were humoring her sense of possession, helping her decide what was properly hers.

"So what is it you're waiting to have settled?" Eddie asked them.

When Grace took him another paper to sign he was as happy to see her as the loan officer at the bank had been. "It's big," she warned. Enough to get construction started on a huge pole barn—more storage—and payment in full on a second truck. Getting positioned to buy other people's hay too, and broker the stuff herself.

"Go to it," her father said, scarcely remarking the notes he was signing.

Ailene had begun a correspondence with a lawyer, an old friend from Roanoke. And Grace saw the collection of things her mother called "mine" growing in the hall. As if gradually stripping the house of furnishings could make Eddie cry uncle. Wedding gifts, the silver, a Mumby print of the Champs-Elysées that had come from Eddie's mother, and any furniture old enough to have dovetail joints.

From the fields Grace watched them filling the big rental trailer that would take it all to Roanoke, relieved that her mother's angry heart must have reached full. Then, the same night, it started all over again. Georgia said, "I think you're right about the porch furniture. It should stay." With that, everything left in the house was up for debate again, and another pile began to accumulate in the hall.

At dinner they were calling their father "he" and "him." "If he doesn't want to talk to us, we'll pretend he isn't here," Ailene said.

"Are you going to leave him his bed?" Grace asked.

"Speaking of beds," Georgia said airily, "where have you been sleeping?" And turning to Ailene, she asked, "Did you know our little farmerette has one of her help staying in the barn?"

"Gorgeous, too," Annalee observed. "Brown as a berry and branded with a diamond."

Ailene could only pretend to be shocked. "How does he eat? Where does he do his toilet?"

Eddie grabbed the table with both hands and shook it until the make-do, jelly-jar water glasses rattled with the surviving motley of stainless ware. At last, Grace thought, but it was only his petulant way of asking silence to say, "The boy doesn't smoke. He's no danger to the barn."

He was taking Grace's part again. "She's running the operation. She can keep anyone she likes here." As if she were owed a liberation in return for her pious use of the family land.

"Quite a turn-on," Georgia persisted, "the Johnson boy."

Billy's unusual friendship with Grace went back to Future Farmers, the club's trip to the exposition in Harrisburg, Pennsylvania, the spring of their junior year. Grace had gone expecting seminars like "The Family Farm: A Revival," at which she and other children of the land would be given a formula. Instead she'd found herself in a huge hall, wandering through rows of equipment—orange machines from Japan promising economies over the famous red or green American tractors. The world out of agricultural balance. Pamphlets showered down, plans for creative financing.

Grace had moved in a hum of subdued voices, a confusion of admiration and despair. Who could afford any of these beautiful things? Nowhere was a secret offered to make things right on a small scale. There were two talks—one on fertilizers, one on insecticides—at which kind and experienced men explained with anecdote and sad countenance, the futility of farming without chemicals.

She went to the convention supper in a big tent and ate barbecued ribs next to the only other girl in the club, who whispered through the speeches that Billy Johnson had got the room next to Grace's in the motor inn and was planning something. That night Billy tried the door between them. Probably startled by how easily it opened, he quietly shut it and went back to bed.

Billy sat next to her on the bus trip home, his way, short of words, of declaring a tentative love for a girl with a body as straight as a boy's and the brass to join a boy's club. She spent most of the ride describing her dream of making a crop that would pay on her family's fields above the river. He could help.

By his third summer working for Grace, Billy was her close friend. He amused himself with several girls in the nearby village, confessing to Grace the little crimes of his roving affection, with shameless allusion to technique, trying to excite her. Accepting her preoccupation with the farm. Taking her firm orders.

When Billy's parents locked the door on him at night he brought his bedroll to Grace's barn. He could have stayed in the house with her father's blessing. Billy shied from that, more comfortable out of sight of the family, though he suggested the trip that could be made between the house and his cozy spot in the loft.

He was the kind of boy who would want her to make the trip. Poor Billy. More and more she was asking special favors of him. Would he mind working on the ground again because Tommer was demanding to drive a tractor. Or Tommer had disappeared somewhere, and would Billy take his shift in the mow?

Easy to see to the heart of Billy's problem. Feckless, handsome. The girls came to him. The one who called and called after watching him take his casual turns in the roller rink. The one who drives to Billy's place from Winchester on the chance he'll come out of the house and get in her car. At his age, already an expert in no-fault romance.

"He's just grazing," Grace assured her mother again. "He wouldn't even stray through an open gate."

The summer took a sour turn. A bad smell in the barn. Inconvenient rain, and some wet bales had gone into storage. A complaint of moldy hay. It was a mistake to put Tommer in charge when Grace went to town on farm business. He wasn't working out. She'd misjudged the wrinkled nose and raised corner of his lip. Not parts of an infectious smile. Rather, a recurring sneer which he turned on other members of the crew.

Shirking heavy work, Tommer had daily reasons for visiting the house—telephone, bathroom. Actually to take another look at Grace's sisters, lovely mysteries to all the boys in the fields by then. Why would married women sit alone all day doing nothing?

There was a week when Grace's father, who hadn't seemed to care what anything cost, was suddenly interested in farm operations again. He came out of the house and lectured her in front of everyone: "Simple physics. Damp bales generate heat. Spontaneous combustion. Poof! You've got a fire."

Grace gave the order. "Shift everything you have to." They had to get down to the bottom layers. A thousand bales sat outside overnight and were drenched by thundershowers, spoiling them for anything but mulch and starving cattle. And fodder for Ailene. Useful in advancing her case against Eddie and the farm.

There was no avoiding Ailene's legal correspondence with her counselor in Roanoke. She left it around for anyone to read. It was no secret the farm had been bought with money that was Eddie's before his marriage. There was a deed in his name. Reassuring, until Grace read a week later that her mother had "certain marital rights in the property. . . . It's hard to believe the bank hasn't asked for your signature on the loans."

The weather stood balancing between the last soft breezes of July and a season of suffocating humidity. Grace entered this part of the summer submissively, the way she might give herself up to a steambath prescribed for health. She soaked in her clothes as her men cured under the sun. The Wilsons' backs had reached the dark complexion of footballs. Billy's diamond was disappearing in bronze. Proud again of their shirtless bodies, they knelt on the wagon bed, at her feet, and did hosannas to their queen of beer and the minimum wage.

Tommer ruined it. Legs spread, hands on his hips, he called the Wilsons "gravel backs," and told everyone to get off their knees. Didn't they know the real women were in the house? Chastened, they turned away from him. She was going to fire Tommer soon as she could replace his haybine with a new one of her own.

More of the lawyer's letterheads, and the drafts left under Grace's nose took a morbid turn. "Absent a will, your dower interest ripening on his death. . . ." Georgia and Annalee would have been reading all this too, their inheritance thrown into doubt by the coming divorce and new liens against the farm. More money flowing into the giant hay shed under construction. Another shiny green machine.

"I want you to like what I'm doing," Grace told her sisters. "All this is yours, too." And Georgia, at last, agreed to give up her vigil and go home. Not Annalee, who was pleading with her mother not to be hasty. Clear to everyone by then that Annalee had nothing to go home to. Making no calls to Roanoke and receiving none.

On Georgia's last evening Ailene took up the new complaint. "I want that boy out of there. Do you hear me, Grace?" A love marshal, alerting all of them again to the sexual spark that could jump the gap between house and barn. Goaded on by Eddie's clucking tongue, she brought out a new letter from Roanoke, smoothed it on the table and began to read a part that seemed to please her:

> What your daughter is doing is not real farming. No one in that part of Virginia is doing real farming. Edward has simply been borrowing against the development value of the land.

Grace remembers standing to counterattack, and sitting a moment later in confusion. Her mother had been talking over them, turning to law. "The bank has been warned," Ailene said, while Eddie, patting his lips with his napkin, prepared the final word: "I should have thought your man in Roanoke would have explained it to you. If the bank asked for your approval now, they'd be admitting the earlier liens were not perfected.

"Ailene," he went on, "you keep getting ready not to go. I unpack your bags and you pack them again. What do you expect Grace to think?"

What each parent was saying to her could be made to sound like love. Her father asking "Isn't this what you've always wanted?" And Ailene tugging on her other sleeve, "Honey, for you it's stay and be damned. Please don't go on with this."

Grace had never fired anyone before. "Services no longer required," were alien words landing in her mouth from a movie or a book, and Tommer's response, ugly as expected. "What would you know about being serviced?" He turned his scorn on Billy and the rest of them standing behind her with their heads down. "Don't you know what she is, you saps?"

When he was gone, her men went out of their way for cheer. Billy assured her "Tommer sucks eggs." They were patting her back as they passed her in the field, and both of the Wilsons had their arms around her on the last wagon ride in the evening. Sympathetic hands fondling a safe pet. Avoiding their awkward touch only seemed to make them more sympathetic.

That night, long after lights out, she returned to the bathroom for a second shower, a preparation. She was turning pink under the prickly, hot spray. Along the back of the tub there was a row of plastic bottles, Annalee's arsenal of scent—shampoo, conditioners, oils. Down the line, sampling each fragrance, she came to a liquid peppermint that made her skin talk back.

She was lathering again. Everywhere. In case he's really the kind to go ranging. Whatever he'll want to do—and it's going to be up to Billy—she doesn't want to repulse him.

Dry and dressed, she lay back in her dark room long enough for her family to uncock ears and drift off again. And down silently, out the door, across to the barn. Grace wanted to take him by surprise, then recover in her own bed. It would be like an outpatient procedure for which she'd bring the anesthesia. She'd snuff out apologies before anyone could speak.

In the new barn she's promised to have a partitioned area for Billy, cat-proof, with cot and blankets. A place to call his own with a solid ladder up to it. No need for a stairway of bales like the one she was climbing to his loft when she heard Annalee overhead: "Oh, the bugs! How can you stand it?"

This was none of Annalee's business—running Billy out of the barn. Grace listened beneath them, waiting for her sister to finish and be gone. Annalee must have been up there for some time. She was chatting with Billy like an old friend, not giving marching orders. She was telling him his hands looked so rough, and how much Grace talked about him, how much Grace depended on him. How he was the stabilizing influence among a crew who, after all, were really children. Billy sounded very pleased. Annalee was going back over their history on the place, back to corn and mallards and children running through the fields.

"We worry about her a lot," she said. "You know she's our youngest, our baby."

"I worry too," Billy said.

"Do you know she's lost a lot of money? Do you know what the real story is here, Billy?"

"I think your mother is leaving Mr. Mason."

"Not that. You see this isn't a real farm. We're just giving Grace time to get it out of her system."

The conversation was slowing down, growing indistinct. Annalee was saying, "No, put it where it won't get hay all over it," and Grace knew the first piece of her sister's clothing had already been removed.

The third cutting of alfalfa lay curing on the ground on the morning Ailene left the farm for good with Annalee. Grace stood dry-eyed as they wept in the driveway, lingering next to the loaded car and trailer, pleading. She could feel her father's gaze from the window watching for any sign of defection. She returned the full pressure of Annalee's embrace as she promised Ailene to be careful.

Annalee persisted to the end, whispering, "Come on, tell me which one is yours." And the crew made an unwitting line-up of suspects against the barn, joking while they waited for lady-boss commands. At last the car was moving down the long, cinder drive, an arm sticking out each side, waving sadly backward.

With her men again, Grace was readying the morning procession of wagons and equipment, giving assignments. Time to start paying off the notes in earnest. No chance of a surplus this year. She's worked hard to get here. On her tractor seat, riding the wagon road between the rolling fields, in a happy, dangerous place between profit and foreclosure, forced at last to steer carefully.

3. CIRCLE OF DUTY

With Ailene gone the path for Grace's descent into hell was cleared. For her partner on the way down she chose Jerry Rice, her equipment dealer's son, a quiet expert in diesel, gasoline, and hydraulics, and a master of baler tension. Seducing Jerry, she found him as careful with her as with the machines. A shy mechanic. If a job called for a torque wrench, Jerry was the kind to ease gently on the handle, not wanting to wring off a bolt or break anything. In fact, wanting to be known as the careful professional he was. Maybe surprised by her direct approach, even amazed by her unrestrained favors, he whispered, "I'll fix you so you stop squeaking." He could have been talking to her wagon wheels. Excited by his mix of sweet and crude, she turned for him.

Jerry came whenever she called, never assuming more than that there was work to be done. He drove straight to the equipment shed, and walked around the problem with his brown eyes cast down. Cautious in his diagnoses, generous with his time. He subtracted labor from his bills and later refused to charge anything at all. When he was finished with a job he tossed his long black hair from his eyes, and looked sadly at his unworthy hands, his black-rimmed nails.

Grace hoped to cure the deference, to bring Jerry out, to have him stand in front of her father with no nervous swallowing or yes-sirs. She wanted to be asked out for beers on Saturday night at Franklin's, the bar across the river where her crew could see what was happening. Too soon for Jerry who thought this was properly a secret.

"My father wouldn't mind," she said.

"What would he say?"

"He'd talk to you about the farm problem in America. Tell you the Romans did it all without subsidies."

Grace took Jerry down the path to the creek, to the pool where her sisters used to take Michael. Luring him into the water where he followed her golden back under the surface and came up with all of her in his arms. And she invited herself to his small house a few miles from hers on the same mail route. To make a casserole that would last him a week.

Jerry was a few years older than she, already married and divorced. And wistful as he explained how he and his wife had wanted children so badly. Their mistake, he said, was letting the doctors into it. Jerry had been told to save up his need and the wife was told to take her temperature. When this failed, the wife said he was shooting blanks, and the doctors took her side. Jerry's count was low.

He confessed that and then tried to make a secret of his special boot, the one with a lift hidden in the heel. This time they undressed in the dark. Afterward, he didn't ask her to leave but she could tell he wanted her out of his bedroom before the sun shone on what they'd done. She left under the moon.

Grace knew his thinking: that there was money here not confessed to, that in her family you could go to college and come home without a trade, that her house had a whole room in it for nothing but books, that she and her father were putting on a little agricultural play, that her farm was not going to last.

For every tractor Jerry's father moved off his lot he was selling thirty-five riding lawnmowers from his showroom. Even he read to her the message written on the landscape—

short grass and small mansions. Didn't hurt him, he said. If the land divided, his customers multiplied. There was more machinery per acre than ever before. Grace was one of his last big-ticket clients. For this she received green-and-yellow baseball hats and toy replicas of her equipment, premiums connecting her to a dwindling brotherhood of farmers.

In late October that year when her haying crew had gone off to school, or to their serious jobs, she had more work for Jerry. Winterizing the equipment, her excuse for bringing him around. As if overhauling, greasing, draining carburetors were essential to the mechanical health of the farm. And Jerry was accommodating, too polite to say, no, this isn't necessary. Besides, he liked taking things apart, on the hunt for a worn belt or bad bearings. In his slow season he was happy with preventive maintenance.

Grace knew he could let this go, give her up if she wasn't making the advances. He wasn't exactly indifferent, but not greedy either. She was charmed as much by his slow, casual criticism as by his silent affection. When he told her, "I believe you've got a little work odor on you," she said, "Let's go wash it off." Proud of her freedom, her wild pursuit of a calm, ordinary man.

He wouldn't spend a night in her house. "My father's very understanding," she told him again.

"He shouldn't be. I'm not taking you in there."

Like that, and then falling so easily to the direction of her hand and lip in his own house. She went on with this as if, through habit, she might bring him into a full and open desire.

Grace was still wheedling to be taken to Franklin's. She went there on her own one night, supposing one of her farm boys would welcome her at his table, but none of her crew was there. And several rheumy old citizens, residents of the river town's dilapidated Y, swivelled in turn on their stools, and stared, one at a time, right through her stony eyes into her lonely heart.

She left the bar, forgetting to tip, and drove to Jerry's place. His lights were out. She woke him and fawned her way again into his bed.

"I don't believe you really want to live here," he said after his pleasure. She slid off into work plans for the winter. When her barn and shed were empty, would he like to travel in the hay truck with her to Pennsylvania and New York to find more for her customers? Maybe the prospect of out-of-county overnights would appeal to him.

"Let's wait and see."

"If you want me again, wake me up."

"I suppose you can sleep here," he said, drowsy, rolling away from her. "I didn't know you were planning on it."

Angling for companionship from a man so willing to let her go, Grace was aware there were two stories here. The one known to her and her family, the way they saw themselves, arriving in this northern reach of the state from a more stylish society. How they practiced their country career, putting their acreage to work with an imported ingenuity. Switching from corn to ducks to alfalfa. As if the fields were the squares of a game that could be won by clever play.

Then the story seen by the natives—people like Jerry and his father, and the farmers already here when the Masons arrived. Practical men, belligerent in their choice of dangerous herbicides, the men selling now because their lives along the river farmland no longer made financial sense. In the Masons they saw privilege and quirks, and a room that held only books. And the black-pajama man who was always in it.

Sliding down further in the bed, nesting the tops of her

feet in Jerry's soles, Grace was aware of trying to make the two stories one, remembering her mother's complaint, "Grace has always tried to climb down from the rest of us." In the early days hadn't she chosen the room off the kitchen for herself, where she could pretend to be hired help rather than family?

Her mother had played good sport to Eddie's changing plans for so many years, and her life had not been unhappy here. If only he hadn't worked so hard at silence in the last year, Ailene might still be on the farm, supporting the next five-year plan and fretting over Grace's casual way with her young work force.

"My mother would have liked you." She was reaching far beyond truth to something wished for, forcing the two stories together once more.

"She isn't dead," Jerry mumbled to the wall.

"I mean if she'd really gotten to know you. You as you are with me. I didn't mean would have liked you, I meant will like you." He was moving closer to the wall.

Perhaps if she could explain to him why her family's livelihood had never seemed to be in question, how it was they could play with their property on whim, as it appeared. Not a question of money so much as attitude. If the truth were known, his father's profit was multiples of the money Eddie or Grace had ever hoped to make here. But Mr. Rice, grandson of native sons, had risen from a field hand to become the local farm-machine man, while Grace's father arrived as recently as twenty-five years ago with some family money in his pocket, and a library.

"You know," she said, "I'm falling behind. Not keeping up with the notes."

"There's more where the other came from ... you can get some of that."

"No, the bank won't move. My mother stopped it."

She was doing spoons against his back and legs. He wouldn't turn. "My mother is going to like you." She wondered at the transparency of her repeated invention, remaking her mother for Jerry though Ailene had so recently gone over to the other side, rejoining what was left of the hotel clique in Roanoke. Thick as thieves again with Aunt Michael.

"All my family would love you once they got to know you." She remembered what Aunt Michael actually said: "This is the way a woman falls."

Even her mother had felt there wasn't quite the right gene pool here to which she should expose her daughters. Salt of the earth all right, but in the end, simply not enough people to make a society. Never a fall or spring cotillion that would have been the girls' birthright in Roanoke. No Christmas Assembly.

Where were the seasonal joys—street carolling, Easter parades, or well-bred Halloween mischief—here next to a village whose chief holiday pride was measured in the number of fire engines and rescue vehicles it could attract from neighboring counties to make Fourth of July bedlam on main street? A pleasure in deafening noise, the sign of a community of tin ears.

Growing up, Grace and her sisters might have thought Roanoke the cultural focus of all the South to hear Aunt Michael tell it. And Ailene hadn't contested this notion, which was based on a handful of events in the salon of their grand hotel—a performance of a famous string quartet, the lecture of an anthropologist, the readings of several forgotten authors, apparently revered for having written no fat or popular books. Distinctions that would only draw Jerry's contempt, and increase his confusion of Grace with the rest of her family.

He had his secrets too, after all. One she'd discovered

while straightening his boots. Surprised by the weight of one, upending it to see what would pour out, and then reaching in to find her hand stopped so abruptly in the heel. Not so big a difference. Less than an inch. She had scattered the boots again before he came out of the bathroom wrapped modestly in his towel. A private truth, better left to the fullness of time.

Next morning, coming home to her farm, she found a large cardboard sign at her river-road entrance. Its black lettering painted crudely: "TITLESS WITCH FARM. SISTERS AVAILABLE. CHILD LABOR WELCOME." Down from her pickup's cab, she tore the thing apart and threw the pieces in the road.

Say nothing. Give no one satisfaction. If she told Jerry, it could only diminish her. He needn't have prejudices reinforced. It must have started with Billy. She sorted through an imagined gallery of leering village faces.

Jerry didn't call that night, or the next, or the next. Other times he could be so thoughtful in the way he shared decision making. Never forcing a point. "We could tear this one down. Get into the transmission." Acknowledging that Grace, too, would recognize a leaking seal. Flattering up to a point.

After dark, the initiative was still hers. "I'm coming over."

"If you like."

"Right now. It's been almost a week."

Her argument with Jerry was the same she was forced to with her mother: "You think I'm something more than I am."

Enough for her that she and Jerry had mutual interest in arable land and the nomenclature of her machines. She knew he was not a prude, knew the coy way he met the stray affection of the waitress in the village lunch room, answering her pleading eyes with a set grin, putting a distance in flirtation.

Grace was climbing down from the place where she supposed he saw her. He was paralyzed, she thought, by imagined inferiority. She ran the dirty sponge over the sticky oilcloth on his kitchen table, then went after the dark stains on the linoleum floor. As she scrubbed she talked about her cousin Michael and the summers on the game farm, thinking the story with its trick ending might separate her, make her a common enough Mason to be trusted. She could explain how the family linen had never been completely white again as far as her aunt was concerned.

Silly not to see that Jerry would put a moral on it, want to know who had been whipped and which parents did the whipping, and whether Grace had been sorry. "We didn't get whippings in our family," she said. "We were always sent to our rooms."

"You were already in your room," he said.

Her stories kept working against her. "You aren't cleaning the floor," Jerry told her very slowly. "You're just washing your hands."

"What do you mean by that?" She threw down the rag.

"I mean, do you care what my kitchen looks like? Or is it just I've got to see you on your knees? I don't want you doing this."

For the time being the cure for an awkward challenge was in the bedroom, and that's where she led him again, thinking once he gets used to this, he'll loosen into the ways of an intimate best friend. She had something different to offer that night, something he wouldn't dare ask for. As if a sexual extravagance could lead to his conversion.

Something fine could still come of all this. Grace felt sure of it. A long, honorable partnership eclipsing the fears of their families. This was only the first stage, and so it might seem ugly and debasing that she could behave this way.

There was a middle land in a month of no restraint when his labors over her tractors must have been suffused with a daily regret that he had not been able, so far, to thank her in kind, moments when his flesh-reveries of her last night's sweet sacrifice must have been confused with the longing for tonight's. She was ready with a whole season of intimate gifts to further amaze him.

"The whole body is the land of love," she remembered her father saying, something useful translated from an ancient language. From night to night in misty dissipation with this as her mantra over the landscape of love. What could be violated when all was licensed? One day, she knows, he'll hear her say something that delights him, and all these gifts will become miracles of graciousness. And he'll be at pains to repay them.

"All right! All right!" he said at the end of that month. "I'll take you to Franklin's. Might as well. Can't dance." A line so overused in this countryside it's almost like breathing. Thus not an invitation after all. More a weary concession, yet something different, with villagers and neighbors welcome to whisper the item into a commonplace. Entering Franklin's together, leaving together.

Over her memory of it is a song. The jukebox was cornered through the night by a single man with a stack of quarters, all of them devoted to one tune, like a musical sympathy card written to his private pain. The evening began with the tall, miserable man leaning over his record, embracing the round shoulders of an old jukebox that pumped red liquid through fat glass tubes. Fed with new coins before the last were digested, it could only return to its one complaint: "Your poison love has stained the lifeblood in my heart and soul, dear."

Grace remembered each detail. In the face of an unconscionable ending, her own heart gave her no choice. No use to her anymore, the lewd particulars of what she'd promised Jerry as he sat fidgeting in the bar, his thumbnail digging away at the beer label. It had only been talk because the night had come to an abrupt halt with him dumping her at the end of her driveway.

Franklin's was already busy when she walked in with him in tow, his eyes cast down, passing people he knew. Of those Grace recognized, there were two young men who had worked for her in her first alfalfa summer, then Wesley Wilson, who had brought his own embarrassment, a beer-drinking minor who left him for Billy Johnson as soon as Billy came in. Beyond Wesley, the regulars from the Y, and at the end of the bar, drinking by himself, Tommer.

He brightened as if his evening's entertainment had arrived. Grace began to work the room with Jerry at her side. She was offering jobs for the next year, joshing and complimenting her old field talent, bragging on them for a past twenty-thousand-bale summer—a summer that had astounded people and made them wonder for a time if she had found a secret that should have been theirs. They had sold, and Grace was still there with her three hundred acres.

Jerry had gotten her away from the others. When Tommer arrived beside them, they were sitting alone. It was loud enough for all to hear, even the tall man taking poisoned love at the jukebox. Tommer attacked him first: "Mister, you've been poisoned a dozen times. It's a wonder you're standing at all." This on his way to their booth, making sure everyone followed his progress down the bar, tweaking an ear, turning Wesley's stool under him, reaching Grace and Jerry as if by accident.

"How's the farm? And look who's here. Your favorite mechanic. Hey, Jerry, I hear you've been tinkering with Grace's parts." Grinning, ready if Jerry moved.

Jerry did nothing. Later, he got up and joined Tommer at the bar, leaving Grace to mix on her own. The two men were joking, poking each other in the shoulder, and she could only imagine them telling stories of insincere and dirty love.

On the way home Jerry spoke of Johnson grass and paraquat, then tried Deere versus Kubota as a topic. At the farm driveway he reached across her and opened the door for her to get out.

Grace had always counted on her father's neglect, first his disregard for her long period of abstinence, then for her season of wandering from her own bed. Now he offered a handkerchief for her misery, and later, his too obvious analysis. "Rural counties aren't equipped for love."

His kind intelligence was worthless to her. What could she expect from a man whose latest passion was his translation of yet another Latin poet? Virgil this time. He was trying to make the *Georgics* fit agriculture in the twentieth-century Piedmont.

He overrode her sorrow with sonorous syllables. ". . . *Redit agricolis labor actus in orbem atque in se sua per vestigia volvitur annus.*"

It sounded to her like a doctor's sterilized naming of body parts and functions. This should help her through a difficult time, he said. "Roughly speaking, it means your farm work returns to you full circle. Just as the year revolves, following in its own footsteps."

Circle of duty? Earth's bounties? Living simply in nature? He must have seen that he was preaching far beyond Grace's achievement. "Virgil had names for your people, Grace.

Your Jerry was his *acer rusticus,* the industrious, shrewd countryman."

"What about Tommer? What would Virgil call him?"

"That's easy. He's the *iratus arater,* the irritated ploughman. Benighted and angry. Burned by the sun. Not exactly 'ate up by ignorance,' as your boys would say, but maybe tormented by it."

For several months Grace had seen so little of her father, they might have been living in separate houses. She'd been out of his sight most of the time, but comforted by predictable noises—the flushing of his toilet at the same time each morning, the opening rattle of his typewriter keys after the popping and sputtering of his percolator. All suggesting a healthy regularity. He was usually in his study before she left for outdoor work.

Coming to him like this in his little workroom in the afternoon was tantamount to asking for a lecture on the relevance of antiquities to her problem. His concern for Jerry somehow turned tragedy into a cyclic certainty—life, struggle, death—broad and useless to the detail of her loss, and launching her father into his own torment of the moment, and Virgil's. How the good earth can turn bad, and not just from drought and pestilence.

Eddie was burrowing further into his own mind, even cursing the infrequent ring of the telephone. Instead of altogether ignoring it, he eased his family conscience, installing an answering machine in case the call from Ailene might come to reform the marriage.

Grace was waiting for a different kind of news. She saw a time coming when she might be landless, but truly rich, floating aimlessly on cash. She became fixed, for no good reason, on the mailbox. Her daily walk to the end of the driveway began with a secret prayer that the continental reach of the U.S. Postal Service might connect her to news that she was still needed in agriculture, that somewhere between shining seas there were fields of grain waving to her. Or, short of this, that Jerry Rice, too shy to state his case in person, might have written a note of reconciliation from as nearby as the village.

Grace knew Jerry was capable of the most ingenuous sentiment. Hadn't she watched him slowly composing apologies to letters from Boys Town, Special Olympics, even CARE, whose children were of a darker skin? Daily the postbox disappointed her, filled only with the sort of mail Jerry had answered, and querulous notes from her mother.

One afternoon there was a fat letter from her lost cousin Michael. By its heft and appearance more official document than letter, written on his university stationery, and so thick the envelope had to be taped shut. His writing was small and legible only after a struggle. The homely scrawl reminded her of the script of a little genius in her high school, a regular volcano of information, too active to concern himself with the cosmetics of his erupting knowledge.

And why all this from Michael? His complete recent history, plus that of the young lady he'd taken up with. Eddie seemed excited by the letter, though the gushing was a bit awkward, something like a child clinging to a stranger's leg when its own parents were in the room.

"Of course, for Michael, they've never really been in the room. How long has it been since we've seen him?"

A few days later, Michael appeared on the place with this new lady friend of his, flushed and eager to show them this Starblanket and to show her the farm. "This is where we used to . . . and this is where we . . . ." Grace remembered how he'd been passed down from one cousin to the next, over the years, like an outgrown toy.

They began to get Michael's history from his own mouth, and from the girl, who was quite beautiful, and disarming, with very specific questions about fertilizer chemistry.

4. STARBLANKET

"Six years ahead in life, six years behind in books." The dean reinstating Michael had predicted malaise. "Keep the blinders on. Keep a tight focus on the required work. I'll have my eye on you." An unpleasant eye, a gray eye grown large and split behind a thick bifocal lens. "And watch out for scholar gypsies. Don't get carried off again."

For a while there had been a small band of young men and women using the university as if it were their club. Intermittently employed, living communally in houses outside Charlottesville, they poached on the campus and its amenities. Never matriculating or paying tuition, they swam in the pool, played on the tennis and squash courts, came to film series, even ate in the cafeteria.

If you went to the right roadhouse on a Friday night you could hear them boast of their latest scam, and listen to their drunken anthem:

> *Whatever we want we take it,*
> *And if there's a law, we break it . . .*

A few of the poachers had forged student cards, though most used friendships in the university community as their cover. Some had gone into the larger lecture halls to take notes, not out of intellectual curiosity so much as the thrill of their growing fraud. A leaky secret that couldn't be kept forever.

By the time Michael arrived for his second go as a freshman, most of them had been scared off, or had drifted away. Toward spring he had hit his stride as a scholar, reached a contented state of mind in which new information fell nicely into place with concept and fact previously filed. The blinders were off now, but so often around him he saw children.

Grinding happily in the library, melding a philosopher's text on laughter with his English instructor's rule, "all humor is born of switched context," he had drifted from the page to a young lady at a video screen across the room. Zoned in earphones, her head cocked to a grainy Gleason film. Another student of comedy?

On scrap paper Michael had written: "I want to work here until six. Will you go with me then for supper in town? Don't answer right away. Michael. P.S. If the answer is no, it could ruin my study time. What I'd like is the possibility of your company in the back of my mind while I work."

"I'll go," she had answered immediately on the back of his note. "Suffer until six. Starblanket."

Later in the restaurant he asked if the name was given or self-styled. She was almost as tall as Michael, with strawberry-blond hair in disarray about her shoulders. There was a single dimple that threw her face quite off balance when she smiled. In a blue man's shirt, snug jeans, and flat, cloth shoes, she was in uniform for the term.

"In fact," Starblanket said, "I have a brother named Catwinkle."

"Your parents were hippies?"

"I think they were there before the word."

Michael had been pleased to be sharing curried tuna with a woman who seemed to be his own age, though her enthusiasm with the food, her order of a second wine spritzer before the first was finished, gave him a turn.

"Did they wreck your face on your I.D.?" He was pulling his student card from his wallet as if an exchange of credentials could have been a social grace.

Would he settle for driver's license and major credit cards? Starblanket Cole of Carlin, Virginia. Her parents' address, she'd said. No longer hers. The license portrait was washed out, owlish. "Me in flu season." Like Michael, she was twenty-four, with lost years to explain. But a senior, she claimed.

"Being careful this time around," he told her. Almost finished as a freshman now with only one more set of marks to put before the dean. Even at this first meeting Star advised him to relax.

"Hang out with the medical students, talk to math professors. Inhale the wide wind of the place. Jump the artificial fences." She called his underbite a strong chin, and asked quite suddenly if he was one of those still living off his parents.

"Not still," he told her. "Again." Since his reformation.

She could show him the way to independence, she said, leaning closer for his reply. Enchanting, her eyes black with mischief, she was sucking the thumb that had stirred her spritzer. She swilled the drink, gobbled the curry. Had to run because her people would miss her. "The ones I live with."

"Three tall men and their ladies," she explained. With machines in the attic that hum long after she falls asleep at night. Her people, she said, were bronzed in all seasons. The women wore startling makeup, and went about the overheated house in spring dresses throughout the year.

She had pulled out all the plastic again, showed how many ways she could pay.

A few days later, Starblanket tapped his shoulder in the cafeteria. Said she'd been working her way through all the *Lucy*'s in the library's television archive. Setting out to prove that a prejudice against TV had kept Lucille Ball off Chaplin's pedestal. An unlikely honors thesis. Too much fun.

He felt himself being drawn away from the safe curriculum again. Unlike the people he'd fallen in with six years earlier, this woman already had a broker. "Don't worry," she told him. "No one invests too much time in me. Your downside risk is slight."

Star's evening was already planned. After an hour with Lucy she'd be ready for her usual run out to the stadium, then off for an "action tub," the whirlpool bath used by Women's Tennis.

"They let you in there?"

A credit card opened the door. If her way was blocked she sometimes settled for a steambath in one of the dorms. "I close the shower room and turn on all the hot taps."

Star was scanning the cafeteria. "Talk to me. Naturally. Talk." She was hiding her face from someone.

Out of the cafeteria, herself again, striding out like an eager scholar to the upper lawn. There, with her sweater for a pillow, she lay back on the grass and told him, "So get it on. Isn't that what your crowd used to say?" She shied from his reaching hand. "Not you. Your story. How come you're six years late?"

"You have to remember," Michael had told her, "in those days we worked on holy futures. In the name of purity we were hollow-eyed with pot, groggy with orgasm. We consumed mysteries of the world in single seminars. Without bathing, we were too clean for this place." He was gone before the end of his first semester.

Six of them had dropped out together, Michael said, heading for Berkeley, but throwing the I Ching too often for it to lead in a straight line. California by way of New Orleans and Missoula.

Starblanket had sat up, maybe leaning toward a half hour with Lucy. "Wait," he said. "I want to tell you how I began to worship a bush."

Michael had been in charge of the group's holiest ark, a small, black film canister filled with cannabis seed. On the way west he would take it from the deep pocket of his overalls and shake it like a shaman's rattle that promised connection with a nurturing plot of land across the continent.

The plot was an abandoned gold claim in Big Oak Flats, where they found two sheds for shelter and a rich, dark soil for the planting. Then the search for work. Michael had become a spademan at a huge nursery, staying long enough to qualify for unemployment, then kicking back as the group's cook and gardener.

In their second California winter they had been full of sickness. Long fevers, projectile vomiting. They heard voices wailing deep in the mine shaft, calling them to a dark end. Michael had been too sick to move. The group had renounced western medicine. No one went for a doctor. Instead they looked for contradictions in his life.

If Zen meant so much to him, he'd been asked, why the vanity of curly hair to his shoulders? With his permission they shaved his head and threw the long black locks onto their compost. The next day he was taking nourishment again, on his feet and nursing a friend through the same deathly flu. By the end of that season they were all bald-headed and much distrusted in the area.

"You couldn't blame people," Star thought. There had been a lot of dangerous monks waiting in the wings. In her case, she said, she'd built counterculture antibodies, exposed to the behavior of outrageous parents, way ahead of their time as hippies.

Whatever she wanted from the university, she was fitting

in in style. Not only the starched clothes and pampered complexion, but the spring in her step as she went from one campus activity to another. A good likeness of a proud and busy student. She even had the little bump on the side of her middle finger where a pencil had rubbed too hard for too long.

"Our résumés wouldn't look good," Star said.

"Anyway, back from near death, with credit to the shorn vanity." He'd been delighted to come upon his hair again that summer, woven into a small nest in the branches of a manzanita bush beside their garden. They stood around it, pointing to the cunning weave without touching.

That season the bush had been their temple. Its bright red bark, small berries, and wiry branches holding the recycled hair. Left to them as a sign. All of them in good health again, on the spiritual path.

Star would listen to Michael's western tales without much enthusiasm, then go running off across the dewy lawn, her destination disguised in the shadows of the colonnade. She'd appear here and there in his academic day without explanation. Just sampling. Following her own advice to relax about course work and absorb the whole university. Better Star appearing next to him for an outdoor class in the amphitheater than the work-shy gum snapper who waited on test days at the door of European History and asked for trends.

Michael could imagine himself transported by Star, carried away from the telltale campus in her shiny Toyota to be instructed in the ways of her other life. When she pulled to the curb in front of the bookstore one morning and said, "Get in," it had been more a piece of mutual engineering than shocking good fortune.

Star announced a picnic catered by Colonel Sanders. "You're invited." Driving north to a deserted river bank, she asked if he knew that a student opening a life policy today could be worth a quarter million at forty-five. How serious was he about his future? And after the picnic had been laid out she began to flash numbers, magically grand, in the liquid crystal of her pocket calculator. They should be looking to their futures while they grazed among professors. "Do you understand?" she'd said. "I'm offering you something only money can buy."

She named three underwriters anyone could trust, and a breath later was going on about Kepler's magic formulas. As if actuarial tables could be used to chart the sweep of planets. Finished with his future, Star had asked politely for more of Michael's past. The years he couldn't put on the résumé. Why had he stayed so long?

The wiles of the one he'd called his lady, a child barely out of high school. "All that," Michael said, "plus I'd been working to become group alchemist, the one with the golden cure for the head."

When the California epoch palled, he'd left his friends in Big Oak Flats, setting off in search of an Indian named Eagle Flight with a wide reputation in herbs. He'd found the medicine man in a dusty camp on the edge of Renson, Nevada.

Michael had been amazed how quickly the Indian drew him inside and questioned him. Did he have a driver's license? Could he hunt rabbits, make a garden in the desert? Would he stay through the moons without whining? Help the wife and child around the house?

Yes, yes, and yes. All for Eagle Flight's instruction.

As it turned out, the herb doctor had no quick recipes for white men. His specifics came after days of meditation and were not revealed in formulas. His first order: "Let your hair grow out and don't bring your marijuana in here."

Starblanket, who seemed so passionate to know all about him, had still been cold to the facts. He wouldn't show her his diary with its monotonous confessions of masturbation, and doggerel, all scattered through with the bar patterns of confuting tosses of the I Ching. He'd preferred to convince with detail—Eagle Flight's missing toe and permanently dilated left pupil.

After six months of trotting at the wise man's heels, and hoping to put himself next to nature in the Indian's eyes, Michael had told him about the nest of his own hair. Never anticipating the way the man would darken and order him away. "You have to get that and bring it to me. It's hurting you."

He'd said it would turn Michael's thought in circles and his life into repeating patterns. But hitchhike five hundred miles back to the manzanita bush on the chance his woven hair would still be there? It was go, Michael realized, or renounce faith. He left the next morning and returned five days later with the nest stuffed in a small box.

Back on campus, Star had been taking Michael over jumps from crystal logic into abstraction, leaving the sidewalks around her sprinkled with names like Santayana and Wittgenstein. "By the way. Did you know Wittgenstein taught machine guns how to fire through the turning blades of airplane propellers without cutting them in half?" None of this proving she was a legitimate undergraduate. He began to stalk her elusive shadow through the colonnades, and saw that the gift of her brief company and financial advice was widely offered.

Star appeared wealthy beyond care, even contemptuous of the struggle Michael had had getting unemployment payments transferred from California to Nevada. She vamped up and down like a woman of a thousand acquaintances and no real friends. He watched from behind a column one afternoon as she accosted student after student on the hillside common, bounding from one prospect to the next as they filed up the brick walks.

It wasn't her natural parents who supported the flamboyant style. The shiny car and the plastic in the folding section of her wallet that fell to her knees like a trick deck of cards. Her people, so generous with money, had her on a short social leash. No overnights. And they didn't want her getting involved with the students she met. It could spoil their interest in her.

Michael couldn't believe it.

It was no more, she observed, than was asked of Miss America. She was grateful for their parietal influence, their gift of forced purity, though she'd worn it more like a scarlet A than a nun's habit.

With the term's end drawing closer, Michael's time had become more valuable. Star said she could introduce him to a new speed-reading technique, show him some mnemonic devices that would help his recall, things that had worked for her. In the meantime, terribly busy, approaching gaily, then sliding off on another hurry-up mission. Flattering though, to be continually reminded of his duty to a future, with its implication that she sometimes imagined herself beneficiary of a shared life.

"We're so far ahead of these kids," she told him. "Nothing to be ashamed of. Nothing to lower our eyes about and pass on opposite sides of the campus paths." It was lubricious children around them who couldn't handle their emotional lives, the ones making themselves miserable with sex given and sex denied.

On a Friday evening, with his weekend mapped for study, Star had come to his room quite forlorn. The world had turned against her. "They're threatening to drop me."

Abruptly, she'd become a disappointment to her adoptive family. Her free spending, which rested on their countersignatures, might be cut off.

Star had begun to mimic a professor, pinching her nose: "I had trouble reading this Lucille Ball thing of yours, Miss Cole."

What had she told him?

"Not to worry. They were doing wonderful things for dyslexia these days."

She was ready to explain things she hadn't had time for before. How she had grown distant from her real parents in Carlin, where a block of tofu could last two weeks if its water was changed daily. They'd confessed that Star's conception was an accident, and her upbringing, a difficult, communal chore.

She'd known a confused discipline in a commune above the Shenandoah River. One group had encouraged her as a small child to cry and babble freely. Others had spanked her hard for disturbing the peace after six P.M. She could remember house meetings at which the Starblanket problem led the agenda.

Once, a young lady assuming parents' privilege had beaten her severely. Star had her fill of the folksy imperative, the soft voices, the pose of endless patience. Her parents had been on their own for ten years now, her father driving the county bookmobile, and her mother at home, picking pests off garden vegetables, and attending to their difficult, healthy diet.

Their outward hippiness had disappeared—the shifts, the sandals, the lowered voices. They were left with only the stainless rectitude. Righteous people, Star said, with no church to vent their virtue. For Star, visiting them had been like going home from a college of liberal arts to a university of the soul. Even the way she breathed was wrong. Inhaling through her mouth.

It came from a fear of smelling the real world, they'd told her. Star had said she used to be afraid to take a boyfriend home to Carlin. Her parents would throw her together in the same room with the boy, as if the house rule were two to a bed.

Even now it was hard for her to go home, she said. Since her regimen of no-romance, her parents could make her feel abnormal, even cheap, still holding out on nature.

If Michael's story was all bogus mysticism to Star, why had she led him on, demanding all of his western adventure? The nest, he said, had been kept in a jalopy until full ceremony could be arranged. Eventually, four people had driven into the desert—Eagle Flight, two of his friends, and Michael. With the nest in its box, and a chicken breast quarter, still under plastic, riding together in the trunk. Michael was asked to help them think their tires would not go flat.

They had stopped in sagebrush country and prepared a cedar fire. The man with the nest had dropped it, let it roll away in the wind. Strands of Michael's untreated hair were escaping across the desert.

Michael had chased and gathered what he could. Eagle Flight straightened each recovered strand, burned them, and fanned the smoke into the chicken. It was an incomplete rite that had left the Indian sullen. Michael said he'd never been the same for the medicine man after that.

There had been the lingering touch of Star's fingers on his arm, and his sense that their histories were flowing together into one story. But next evening there she was again, parading outside the dining hall, bearding young men with good cheer and a mind to their nonexistent portfolios. If she hadn't been so flashy, they'd have been calling her names worse than nuisance.

Star had turned and come back on him. "As for you," she said, chucking him under the chin, "I want to take you home tonight. Relax. When we get there I'll take you right upstairs." She'd led him away with a warm hand.

What would her friends say?

"The usual. That you're not worth it. My future's too bright to let one man steal me."

She'd driven the car slowly, far west of the town, this way and that on narrow roads until he was lost. She'd had another fact-of-the-day for him. "It's no accident the seventeen-year locust chose a prime number. It escapes dozens of predators whose life cycles might otherwise intersect more often with its own."

He was lost and she was home. A big three-story house in the woods. And Star's people were just as she'd reported. Health by Nautilus and tanning closet. Various colognes competing for attention. College souvenirs all around. Decals, T-shirts, sweatshirts, miniature basketballs, beer mugs, lamp shades, notepaper. The house littered with the logo and pet name for the alma mater that had never been theirs.

They were expecting him, drinks in hand. They knew all about Michael and his medicine man. If he could just sit down for a few minutes, someone was upstairs tidying up, getting the room ready for them.

"I'm going to show you the rest," Star whispered, his exit blocked by her friends' graciousness. A moment later she was prodding him gently up the steps. They were moving along a hall of bedroom doors, then up another flight to a wide-open area bathed in fluorescent light.

Computer terminals all around, one wall solid with filing cabinets. A man sat alone in the middle watching numbers squirt onto a spreadsheet. He swivelled and said, "Hello, Michael," and began to tick off names that had made Hartford a proud capital—any of which he could trust. Star was backing away down the stairs.

There had been a little scene. The man went on for a half hour or more, his smooth presentation so full of "hopefully" that Michael, before declaring no interest, helped him with grammar. "A smart ass. Why do you people come here wasting our time?"

On the way back, when he'd called her tactic entrapment, Star had driven on without argument. In the dark she took a hand from the wheel and touched his cheek with the soft fingers of a blind woman reading a face. "Don't be angry." She said she was proud of Michael. The way he'd stood up to them.

They stopped at a restaurant where beef was called "turf," and Star had confessed to full-time poaching with this practicum of her own in business. Contrite, she was ready to submit to more hippie tales.

Michael turned back to his last days in the West. There had been another curious fever. Tired of the illnesses, Eagle Flight had pointed him toward the hot waters of Southern California. "He told me to cure myself. He could never make me a whole person."

Michael had tried the Indian's latest—dried jimson weed, the needles of a dog cactus, ground together with a clay pestle, the mixture to be held for several minutes on the tongue while swallowing all saliva flowing from the sides of the burning mouth. This had not helped as he drifted, his bedroll soaked each night in the sweat of intermittent fevers.

Nothing Eagle Flight taught him had worked. Emaciated, a shadow with a thumb stuck out over the pavement, he arrived in San Jacinto, his breath rattling through a thick, dark mucus. Leaning against a phone booth, he found Physicians in the Yellow Pages, then M.D.s, then Internists. That afternoon he began to feed on a canister of tetracycline the old-fashioned way. "Three times a day with meals."

Star was delighted, embracing his return from Indian territory, kissing the final words of conversion on his lips. "I'm going home to Carlin the weekend before exams," she said. "I want you to come with me." Smiling beautifully into a distance that might once again be taken for their linked future.

In his last week for study she was continually coming to his room, pulling him back from the hard edge of scholarly zeal. Reminding him of their superiority over the required course work. Inviting him to range with her to lectures on deconstruction, the red shift, asymptotes.

"What's an asymptote?" he asked her, and for a moment she seemed stumped.

"Think of it this way," she said. "Imagine I was a point coming closer and closer to you. But the formula I'd been assigned never quite allowed me to touch you."

When she wasn't in his room, Star was on the house phone to him, planning the wonderful weekend. And now each time she saw him she had presents. Wild flowers for him to press in the pages of his books, a miniature music box that played five notes, a clear marble with a red core. Gifts small enough to mean everything.

"The wriggling worm has many hearts," she told him. And invited him to prove it as she had for herself under a microscope in the biology lab. In a prickly heat, he saw again that she'd been using the university to far better advantage. Sparkling with curiosity, she'd gathered knowledge that made his effort seem cramped and pathetic, and made his Indian a seedy charlatan in the desert. Eagle Flight's auguries had only reached to the sun and moon and into the center of the earth. What were these against a marble, a music box, a cut flower, all pointing into the realm of one expanding heart?

Friday morning Star had parked again in front of his dormitory, engine running, impatient to be away. Minutes later she was steering them north, Michael and all his texts on the seat beside her. She was looking down at the wall of words and numbers that separated them on the seat.

"What's this?" she said, wrinkling her nose, lifting a calculus workbook with two dainty fingers. Michael took it from her and tossed it out the window. Leaving European History next on the pile. He threw that out too.

Already the trip was stretching beyond a reckless weekend into a grand open-ended truancy. A visit to his cousin's farm on the Potomac. A side trip to the hot baths at Berkeley Springs where they would float together in one of the family tubs. But first a night together in Carlin, a night her mother and father could admire.

Star was talking about graduate work for the next fall. Michael could remember exactly how long it had been since anything like this had happened to him. Six years since he'd pillowed the shame of retreat from scholarship against the easy shoulders of flower children.

By the time they passed under the interstate all academic ballast had been dropped. Moving beyond the university's gravity, he was astonished not so much by his new renunciation of required reading as by his low-class littering of the highway.

5. ENCLOSURE

At the front of the café three tables were always pushed together. A compatible company of thirty or forty men took
luncheon turns at the eight places set there, depending on
who happened to be in the village at noon. They were the
remaining farmers and those of an earlier day, and the supply
clerks, a few seed and fertilizer people, and all welcomed
Grace to join them when she was there.

This board of directors, as the group was called, held in
contempt the town council, for foot-dragging, preservationist,
antidevelopment, and ecological sentiment. The unelected
board had undergone a silent and invisible change. Same vi-
sored caps, same shirts, pants, and coveralls on the regulars,
but extraordinary new wealth.

On a Friday, three months after Jerry's disappearance
from her life, Grace came to town to ask for more time on her
seed and fertilizer debt, and the board called her to join them.
They made an extra place, and she sat wedged between two
fully disguised rich men with bad teeth who had sold their
farmland for new lives. Counting further around she was
aware that she sat with at least four recently made
millionaires.

"What brings you in, young lady?"

She told them proudly of the financial strain of her war
on fungus and weevils.

Alfalfa was a lot of work just for hay, they agreed, and
not as much in demand. These were men who had come up
the country way with Jerry, and were not used to their early
retirements.

Mr. Rice would sit here on occasion. And sometimes

Tommer. There were days when she walked by the restaurant window and saw Jerry and Tommer together smirking, and again she imagined herself as Jerry's dirty story. She supposed they thought of her now as thin and broken, an anxious sexual reed, used and discarded.

The newly rich men did not speak as much as they used to, or as loudly. An advantage had gone out of their banter. No way left to blame their slow lives on wherewithal. A little embarrassed by all the cash they were not inclined to invest or spend. They were living for the time in the same houses, eating the same weekly lunches that circled back to swiss steak on Fridays, when Grace came into town to do her business. By the shifting colors of the county development map they followed the rising fortunes of their neighbors.

They all knew the bank was having trouble with the Mason account. A case of negligence. Loaning money to Grace on her father's signature alone. She wiped the gravy from her plate with a roll, looked up and around the table, and announced the availability of field work in the coming summer. The men might want to pass the news on to their sons.

"Usual benefits?" someone asked her.

"Those men don't think we're going to make it," she told her father. "They think we're selling, too."

"We are," he said. "Your mother is forcing our hand."

He would have battled any threat to the farm in the early years. Once, in a billing argument with the electric company, he had threatened to tell all the world how to make their meters run backward. As a little girl, Grace had been sure he saved them from pitch-black nights. Later, she realized it would have been Ailene, sitting down to write a check, who brought the lights on.

Grace and her sisters had made their father a magician.

And even Ailene couldn't deny she'd admired the show. They'd all seemed to think loaves could be extruded for their sustenance from Eddie's cunning. Tricks for his city ladies. He'd made corn tassel, ducks hatch, alfalfa sprout. But for his next stunt, he was going to pull the carpet of alfalfa from under Grace's feet so quickly she'd be left standing upright, her eyes blinking at a shiny, new landscape.

"This is the deal your mother proposes. We keep the house and barn and seven acres. Enough for our immediate aesthetics as she says. The rest has to go. She wants it shared equally among you, me, her, and your sisters."

If they didn't agree?

"She'll fight to have everything sold. Including the house. She'll set up a trust for you and Annalee and Georgia. Of course, I'd be expected to do the same."

"What's happening?"

"We're all going to be rich. And let's not blame anyone."

Her father had his hands cupped, pulling against each other, taking his exercise from dynamic tension as he remade their world. "Those men won't matter much longer. They're taking themselves out of the picture."

"Sweetie, what's happened here?"

A surprise visit from her mother, who gathered Grace in her arms. "How did you get involved with that man in the first place? Why did you let them cut your hair like that? How did your father get so thin? What are those horrid piles of dirt?

"I hope you're not blaming yourself, honey. It couldn't have been your fault. Why aren't you answering the telephone? Why aren't you answering our letters? Does your father eat regular meals? Why did he let them take down the trees along the road? You should make him shave."

She turned to Eddie and kissed the stubbled cheek. In this transition, Grace said, it was the hundreds of little piles of earth all over the cleared fields that most upset him. Like a groundhog infestation. Actually, holes dug where water would be poured to see how fast it disappeared—tests to prove the coming sewage would sink.

"You'll be glad to know," he told Ailene, "every site perked."

"Eddie, you weren't rude to them? Grace, was he rude to the inspectors? Honey, the farm just wasn't making sense." Her talk for the moment was all about land and development, inevitable change, the hopeless situation in the region. And at that moment, again in her mother's embrace, Grace felt no resentment.

That night Ailene attacked. "I blame you, Eddie. You encourage her with all the Latin hocus-pocus."

Grace called down from her room for them to quiet down. Her mother was asking if he got some kind of thrill from his daughter's extravagant life. This and the dirty Latin. Ailene meant all the loose translations. Authorizing behavior by translating it from an earlier civilization's poetry.

Grace could remember one line in particular: "The habit of intimacy practiced on a man without restraint becomes, itself, an aphrodisiac." Her persistence on the land, her persistence in or out of love, all consistent with Eddie's teaching, according to her mother.

Ailene only stayed one day. The bulldozers had rattled her nerves as they scraped clean the rubble of old fence rows where sumac and ailanthus seemed to grow directly out of fallen rock. There had been no need to mend fences that only enclosed hay fields.

A team in a van came with a transit and fluorescent red-and-orange ribbon that they tied to stakes, revealing a pattern for maximum return from the land. The boundaries of three-, four-, and five-acre lots. Rectangles, squares, some trapezoids, the more awkward shapes forced by surrounding property lines and the adjacent roads.

In the middle of the developer's geometry, the old house remained with the barn and seven buffering acres, and an easement down to the road. Grace and her father watched the building process repeated sixty-seven times, from the excavation of basements and septic fields to the nail tap of the finish carpenters. Sixty-seven wells dug in two years, and more than a dozen dry holes. The din ran dawn to dusk through a summer and winter.

Each lot was surrounded by a black, board fence before the new houses appeared.

"They can't make us do it."

"When it's all around you, it looks like you did it yourself." They were going to be shape number sixty-eight. A square pan, Eddie said, with a curved dent where the property touched the river, and a long handle, the driveway.

Ailene said it was morbid for them to sit and watch it happen. Her letters were frequent and all of one purpose—to move Grace out of the old house where they were squatting in a kind of defiant mourning.

Grace Dear,

Why don't you just come for a visit and try it out here? It's not so old-fashioned as your father pretends. There are people fighting for things you'd like.

Grace supposed she meant more curly black hair beside straight blond in the schools.

Your Aunt Michael has met a Portuguese man. No one can pronounce his name to his satisfaction. We hardly ever go to the hotel anymore.

So now Michael's mother was "Aunt Michael" in the family. Appropriate enough, Grace thought. There was more about her aunt's Portuguese caller, and then:

Let me catch you up on your cousin. He's still in Charlottesville, hovering around the university with the same young woman. God knows what they live on. Let me give you some advice, don't invite them up there again. Your sisters have been quite sweet to Michael. Please answer their letters. And this one. After all, I am

Your Mum

Grace answered, "Daddy's teaching me more Latin. Actually fun. Can you believe it?" She'd begun, Grace wrote, to appreciate the way her father could take long trips, just in his head, across time and oceans. "About the place, you wouldn't like to see what's happening now."

Cement trucks, gravel trucks, graders. The vans of electricians, plumbers, dry-wall, heat-pump people. Carpet and tile experts. Hustling over the small mansions of brick or German siding, or combinations. A lot of the homes had two-story columns in front, holding up suggestions of porches. All this, the daily parade, for Grace and her father.

Grace was half-pleased with the accuracy of her father's forecast of the sudden community around them. Making a Polaroid postcard of one artificial façade, she used it as a little reminder mailed to Roanoke. "Thirty sold, thirty-seven to go. Welcome Wagon busy."

The card came right back, a second message overlaid. "This looks nice. Maybe Eddie should consider something like it before they're all gone. Ease of maintenance is something everyone has to consider eventually."

Grace still believed her parents might find a way to civility and reunion. In this time of fractured estate and delicate feeling, perhaps it would be better to use the telephone than mail. Less chance of misunderstanding. If her mother could only get past that quavering voice of hers to the subtleties of compromise.

Grace had begun to call Ailene from time to time to let her know how truly content she'd become here without the farm. Hard for her mother to accept that a girl who'd refused to go to community college could now be fascinated by declensions and conjugations, all tedious puzzle solving in Ailene's estimation. What could Eddie be leading her daughter toward now, what message at the end of the Latin cryptogram? Only yesterday, worried about baler tension, and today, telling her mother: "Daddy thinks the translators have gotten it all wrong. Trying to outdo each other with casual lingo. Trying to be one of the boys. Why not let these poets be the prissy types they probably were?"

"Grace, are you listening to me? Has he been reading to you about that Gellius, the one who gets so thin from all the perversity?"

Her mother's voice could get so panicky over the Latin thing. And she worried that Grace might get herself into another behind-the-fence affair. "You're well rid of the last one, dear. I hope you'll find something that suits you, and take your time about a man."

"Mother, relax about me. I'm home. It's your home too, don't forget. And I'm not getting a job because, remember, none of us needs the money. Why don't you try to think of this as the year you wanted me to have abroad? Imagine me in an antique land."

"Grace, don't be arch. There was no way the farm could go on as it was. Your father said he'd explained the figures for you. I'm sure it's going to look better after the new people get going with their landscaping. Grace, are you thinking of the boy, darling?"

Grace felt a duty to stay and experience what the sale of the farm had left. For her father this was more like keeping faith with the past, holding a small nation's high ground against the prospect of annihilation. This is the territory of his children when young, of Ailene in rebellion from Roanoke, of himself as a homesteader. For Grace, annihilation was dogwood, spruce, and yew, settled around with pine-bark mulch.

As she talked with her mother, Grace thought of her new community. Sixty-seven new front doors. Not the kind where you could ask for a cup of sugar, but these homes have back doors, too, places where the younger boys who used to come to her in the summers could go to ask for yard work. Really a full trick-or-treat community. And entranceways where expensive wreaths would be hung, suitable for carolling.

Grace had been given comforting news. Something one of the Wilsons passed on to her. Jerry had told him, "She could break your heart just by the way she turned her head."

She walked the perimeter of black, board fence around her seven overgrown acres, trying to rebuild the fallen forest in her imagination, the canopy of trees that had covered their first casual walk to the creek, where she had dared Jerry's full inspection, stepping out of her clothes and wading before him into the deeper water.

The trees beyond were gone, and the naked creek and lowland had the name of a nuisance to the developer—a little floodplain that ran into the larger floodplain of the river. Thousands of square yards of earth had to be rearranged. Standing by the fence in the third spring of Mason Hills, her day-dreaming muddled by the little more than a million dollars that had arrived in her own account, clear of all liens and taxes, she watched someone coming toward her on a miniature green tractor, like a man on a toy, and leaving a miniature swathe of short grass behind him.

They must know how idiotic they appeared, these men on their riding mowers. Sitting boldly, as if on top of several hundred horsepower, spewing puny clippings to one side. The little machine, Mr. Rice's brand by its coloring, turned a corner and faced her. The man gave a small wave, a quick turn of the wrist. Tommer.

Grace moved quickly toward the house. The whine of the little engine increased. Close to her porch, she turned and saw that he was stopped beside the fence where she'd been standing. He waved again, threw the baby tractor into gear, and went on.

Her father was on the telephone in the front hall. "Your mother's on the other end. We're having an argument. What is it?"

"Tommer's back. He's mowing the next place."

That could wait. Eddie wanted her to join the conversation. "Let's give your mother a chance at both of us." His hand covering the mouthpiece, he motioned her down the hall toward the kitchen phone.

"Is that you, Grace? Did I hear you yelling bloody murder? Is everything all right?"

It wasn't long before she was frozen out of the discussion. "Don't leave, Grace. Are you still there?"

She listened with nothing but her breathing and an occasional deep sigh to prove her attention to a debate that was circling around her without inviting her opinion. Why was she staying on a farm where there was nothing left to harvest but a lawn? And they weren't even doing that. Their neighbors were taking them and their little wilderness to court.

"Eddie, it doesn't make sense. Before you can be nostalgic there has to be something worth missing."

Not necessarily, her father argued. According to him, even the most impoverished childhood could be evoked in teary memory, simply because it is yours and because it has passed.

"It's worth missing?" Ailene asked. "So miss it."

Grace trusted her father in this, and more. That when a family split apart, as in a physical experiment, the parts were not lost. Whatever had been given off—heat, broken hearts, tangible property—was capable of recombining. There could be meetings, talking, restoration of the house as it was, social gatherings.

Held by her father's voice and her mother's temporary submission, Grace stopped making faces into the phone. He had never gone on this way, painting himself as curator by default of the family museum, keeper of their past. He would never let the house go as long as there was breath in him.

She could strip the place bare, he said, and this would never change. The house would always be vault of the family's secrets and memories. Don't get him wrong, he said, this wasn't martyrdom. More like a comforting duty. He was happy in his daily routine. And Grace, too, was learning a useful idleness, gaining an appreciation of the cunning tangle of related languages. "I give her a little class each morning."

"Isn't she still on the line? Can't she speak for herself?"

"I'm here. Go ahead, Daddy."

"A vault?" her mother said. "Like a mausoleum?"

No, the rewards lay ahead in a softer future, he said. When the other children came home again, they would open a door, turn on a hall light, run a bathroom tap, and bring on the flood of their recollected youth. A wonderful, happy time for all of them. "As long as the place is here, you'll make the pilgrimage."

Her father's expansive mood led Grace through the house, floating within the walls of bedrooms and bathrooms that had given privacy to the pleasures and disasters of childhood: the inspection of her slowly changing body in front of mirrors, night spying on Georgia's autoerotic moaning, games of sardines ending in the half closet under the stairs before any of them realized that bodies squeezed together with those of neighbor children could be anything more than uncomfortable, and eavesdropping on her mother's continual, long-distance debates with Aunt Michael in Roanoke—conversations that somehow made moral issues out of things like what to wear and where to live. And, at the end of childhood, her mother's discovery of Michael in her room.

Grace was still moving through the child-spy recall of her only home: where to go on the second floor to hear voices from the kitchen, where to stand on a rise outside to see through her parents' bedroom all the way into their bathroom, how the thumping on a rain barrel outside could reverberate through a drainpipe and make a child behind the attic knee wall think she was protecting herself from thunder and lightning.

As her father went on, Tommer came into view in the kitchen window. He was making smaller and smaller rectangles in the neighboring yard, snatching the wheel expertly, making sharp corners, proud, it seemed, of his perfect control over his green design.

Two days later, Tommer showed up again, this time cutting diagonal stripes for the new people behind the western fence—the family just arrived from Alexandria. Perfectly in character. Wasn't it just like him to take wages for younger men's work, to get cute with the patterns he made in people's yards, to wave and flaunt his presence, knowing that it might disgust or frighten them. He was coming close as he could, even working along the fence, trimming with a machine that whirled plastic string, actually violating her line, cutting some of her place.

Later, Tommer appeared mowing the property behind them. He had completely surrounded Grace with his contracts for yard work in the new development. There was still the short border where she could go to sit by herself, protected by the river bank from the sight and sound of his mowing machine. But by the next Labor Day he had appeared here too, floating past on an inner tube in a party of beer, fishing lines, and rowboats, in the middle of drifting laughter, rowdy and lewd. Lying across his tube, he took long strokes that held him for a moment in front of Grace until the current pulled him away.

"Within his riparian rights," her father said. "If he starts up the bank, that's something else."

In the water Tommer had only made an ass of himself. It was when he was alone, hanging on the fences around her, that Grace believed he must be studying how to deal with her. More likely, Eddie thought, he was waiting for the chance to ask if he could cut their grass.

Immediately after the sale, they had let the place run to a motley of weeds, the wild planting of the Virginia wind and roots that creep. Volunteering crabgrass, plantains, orchard grass, scattered clover and rye were eventually covered over with taller things that bloomed in many colors. Yellow field cress, the blue devil, thistle, white-and-yellow field daisies, Queen Anne's lace, and orange ditch lilies along the driveway. And rising above these came locust shoots, volunteer maple, ailanthus, and the soft but rapid sumac, with honeysuckle and poison ivy rampant.

It was nature's landscaping and her father's pleasure, a habitat for birds and small animals. Not at all the scenery preferred by the neighbors for the oldest home among them, and after which the development had been named. Mason Hills. Two stones, each carved with the name, had been set into a pair of short, curved walls of white brick on either side of a paved entrance road that ran up between the new houses. These brick walls, connected to nothing, made only a funnelling target for the new settlers' cars.

As the wilderness grew around them, Grace and her father could take less notice of the mannered estates on all sides. By the third summer of their "lawn-neglect," the term used by the legal posse surrounding them, a mower would have been useless. The healthy jungle they protected with defiant inattention was closing in, well above eye-level, and vines of varied leaf had taken a stranglehold on the house's gutters and downspouts, and were climbing over the barn. How could they be ordered to mow a lawn that was actually more like a forest?

Tommer had clients all over Mason Hills by then, his work completely removed now from their sight by the thickening vegetation which, they argued, it was not only their right but their duty to maintain. For the wildlife, a much needed preserve in this new, outer suburbia.

Picking her way across the property on a September morning, Grace was not startled by the rabbits, a groundhog, possum, squirrels, or even a red fox. This was morning recess from a translation of a Latin poem which, her father said, no one had gotten right. He, too, had failed to bring it into impartial English. The qualification needed to pull it up from simple woman-bashing had become too cumbersome.

Flattering to Grace. The notion that she might be capable

of a language skill her father lacked. The poem was unkind, Grace thought, unworthy of their struggle with it. The first few lines stuck to her tongue with an unpleasant flavor as she left the house for her walk through the undergrowth, repeating her father's version.

> *Hello, darling!*
> *Hasn't your nose grown?*
> *Or am I wrong,*
> *And it's your head*
> *That's getting smaller?*

Why forgive the poet his nasty streak? She was going to tell her father the lines were beyond repair. Grace looked up, and waiting in front of her, leaning on the fence, was an old man. His white hair was clipped short and tidy, and he wore a tie of dark blue around the sagging collar of a white shirt. He looked like Tommer grown old and tired.

"No, please come here," he called. The man was holding the loose flesh under his Adam's apple between a thumb and forefinger, like an appendage meant for steadying his shaky head.

"Your daddy used to have a tarpaulin beside his barn," he said.

"Yes?"

"It was just sitting there for a long time." His eyes were cast down. "I took it."

"Please, it's all right, you can bring it back if you like."

"No." He would not be comforted. "It's torn, ruined. I took it fifteen years ago."

He said he was testifying to all he had done wrong in Virginia. The Lord's pasture was being scraped bald and brown in this area. And some of his old sins had come to the surface, in open view of God and man. The tarpaulin itself had been thrown up from the past onto his ledger with the Lord, when it fouled the shaft of his own bush-hog. And his son Tommer had broken one of his smaller mowing machines when it struck the fallen axle of a derelict haywagon. The wagon, another theft of a slier season.

His voice had steadied, and with a jaw-jutting rectitude he was smiling toward heaven. Tommer, he said, had started reading with him from the book.

Michael had let a whole year pass before writing a bread-and-butter letter. As if his visit to the farm with Star had been a week ago. No apology. Pleasing Grace in a way with its implication that his affection was timeless and without convention. What began as a thank you turned into open-hearted discussion of family. One rambling paragraph:

Your mother says I wouldn't recognize the place now. She calls from time to time with a little have-you-heard-from-Grace panic in her voice. Full of concern for me. Wants to know if there's anything she can do to help me get reinstated. I told her it's better here as a poacher. Actually, I'm a messenger for the university now, and no-body cares if I sit in on a few classes. Star is still doing it her way with wigs and disguises and her own kind of scattershot charm. In the big lecture classes no one has-sles her. They're probably grateful for anyone paying at-tention. There's a little contest going on between her and the campus plainclothesman. He caught her in the dining hall, and said, next time, prosecution. They're fussier about stolen French toast and mystery meat than their professors' ideas. Reason enough for her elaborate dis-guises. My mother is still being rude. When Star answers her calls, my mother says, "I didn't know he could afford a cleaning lady." Georgia and Annalee have been here to the apartment several times. Never together, though usually on the same ostensible mission. To rescue me from the dangerous influence of Star before I'm too far gone to catch up with my honestly employed generation. But hard for them to preach from the pulpits of their found millions. From childhood, I've lumped your sisters together. From those summers when I felt betrayed. I think of it as Georgia dropping me into Annalee's lap, and Annalee passing me on to you. And you, bless your heart . . . . For me they were faithless egotists. And now they're propagandists. So why do I love and admire them while wanting so much to tear away all the authority in their professed calm? Why do I want to see them naked in the wading pool again? Of course, Annalee always argues from the last book she's read, while Georgia lectures from the platform of family pride and honor. They appear to be working on my case, my doomed life with Star, but what they're all really angling for is you, Grace. Your mother, especially. They all think I have a direct line into your willful head. That if I gave the nod, you might take up with "the farm help" again. And you know they'd rather have me raise an eyebrow. They see me as useful, but only at a distance from the farm. Because they wouldn't trust us not to drop everything and run off to the barn. If I hung the moon for you, I could also put out the light. Are you going to travel with your money?

Grace read the letter over several times for some pleasure she might have missed. There was no hurry to answer. After so long a silence, a quick response could only be a reproach.

6. FARM USE ONLY

Tommer still showed himself frequently along Grace's fence lines after his lawn work in the surrounding yards. The menacing leer had given way to a beatific, searching countenance. Sometimes he motioned to Grace to come and join him. She was repelled by the unctuous, country-boy pose, the way, after motioning to her, he would lower his eyes in disingenuous modesty, but there was no avoiding this man. He was doing what he could to put himself in her path, even climbing over the fence one afternoon and coming toward her. Grace retreated into the house, went to her father, and asked if there were shotgun shells at hand. Yes, in the drawer of the hallway table. Tommer had already climbed back into neutral territory.

A week later he walked right up to her in the village with this new open-faced rapture, and extended his hand as if surrendering to a natural comity requiring that she share his bliss. She shook his hand but could think of nothing more to say than that it was a fair day.

"Yes, and look who made it." Beaming with his fresh discovery.

Does he get over to Franklin's anymore? Never. Does he see much of Jerry? Hardly at all. Drink or smoke? No, he serves the Lord now. He didn't just answer the questions, he asked them for her.

Only a quarter hour later she saw him on a bench in front of the hardware, pausing beside his sandwich and soda, head bowed and hands together in a long, public moment of prayer. For Grace he was like a thorn gone from the underbrush, a man neutered, fixed once and forever. Without the wit to hide his alteration from the community. Alone on the bench, he disgusted Grace, he delighted Grace. Out of combat. He probably wouldn't raise his rifle at a squirrel now without weighing the action on almighty scales.

Jerry approached her in the village too, of all things, and asked for a night meeting when they could talk about what had happened and what they should do about it. An odd way of putting this, she thought. What we should do about it. They were going to do something together? About it? She took "it" to mean his recognition of the suffering and injustice he'd caused, and his shameful silence. What had he been doing all these seasons, the shy fornicator? Accepting other work, she supposed, then retreating just as he had from her. Perhaps the bank of county favors had come to recognize that his stealthy night deposits were actually withdrawals. No more automatic tellers serving Jerry Rice's pickup.

"Grace," he reminded her that night, "it was hardly ever my truck, it was yours. And it wasn't your driveway, it was mine."

This time they were in his living room at his invitation. Quite unlike him to be engineering the sexual preparation. "Would you like to see what's under this?" Plucking at his shirt, then his trousers.

"Jerry," she told him, poking him in his naked ribs, "we're not doing this in the shadows anymore."

"All right, let's leave the light on."

And they did, rolling under the glare of a bare bulb that dangled on a cord from the ceiling.

"You won't leave me hanging this time?" she asked.

"Oh no, we'll get the job done."

He wasn't this obtuse. She knew that. Just his way of teasing, his native manner, taking her long-term fear and contracting it to fit the pleasurable moment. He slowed into a rhythm that pleased her, something one might dance to, though now she felt like talking and provoking him. Couldn't afford to enjoy herself, though all the equipment was working, well lubricated, reaping its own pleasure while her mind was busy with the likelihood of another abandonment.

"Tell me about your shoes," she said. While the center held, Jerry had gone ranging with his hands from shoulder to thigh, front and back. Checking out her parts? She should ask him that, too.

"That's right," he said, without interrupting his gentle work.

"We could talk about it later."

"Now is fine. Let's talk about it now." She offered no faint moaning, no fillip calculated to raise his heat. He must have realized he was alone. Grace felt he had put his casual motion on automatic just as she had.

"If you want to know, my right leg is one-half inch shorter than my left. The lift in the boot brings it up to level. Otherwise, I get the sciatica. If you ever had it, the pain shoots down your whole leg." He could have been chatting over coffee. "The doctor gets you up on the table, takes his steel tape and measures from the hip joint to your ankle bone. It's only accurate plus or minus a quarter inch. So the worst I could have is a three-quarter-inch problem. With the shoe, I'm only correcting for the half inch."

"I think it's quite common," she said. Grace thought of the girl with the growing nose, or was it a shrinking head, and of her own life circumscribed by the black, board fence and effete translations, and she stopped moving altogether.

Jerry pulled away from her. "I don't think you understand," he said. "What I'm trying to tell you is we could be married."

Grace didn't realize she was using Jerry's underpants to

wipe her tears away—the first thing handy. He was telling her what they could do with their life together. Custom farming. They had all the equipment they needed: bailers, rakes, combines, ensilage wagons, whatever a land-poor farmer would need, all available secondhand from Jerry's father. Jerry would keep it all running, and she could organize the crews, taking them west and south down the valley as far as need be to find fields under cultivation.

A day later they were making wedding plans. For his family's sake the ceremony ought to be in their church. That would be the big, brown Methodist stonepile in the center of the village. She'll do it there if he'll agree to a reception at her place. Her father would like that. An excuse to bring the family together again on the farm. A great party in her barn. A barn dance. Square, contra, reels, whatever people are doing these days.

Remember, he might not be able to give her children. She told him not to worry, they'd have children one way or another. She'd work on him in ways he hadn't seen yet. And if that didn't do the job, they'd go out and look for a stray or two. Grace, in love, delighted in his dignity, his indifference to her family's pride, and the charm of his ease with his own wit and ignorance.

Grace imagined a family gathering in the church, then everybody they could think of invited to the barn, all the young men who had ever worked for her, friends from high school days. For that matter, everybody in Mason Hills. A blanket invitation to all residents in the sixty-seven new houses around her, even the group that had sued to have her yard trimmed.

Jerry was driving very fast over a dirt road, sliding

around corners. They couldn't wait to tell someone. No lingering engagement. It had to happen soon, before a mind could be changed. With her world transformed in a day, her demon exorcised and her man gone down to his knee, Grace was singing:

> *I want to be a cowboy's sweetheart,*
> *I want to learn to rope and ride,*

wishing she could yodel like Patsy Montana, though her own open range might be small squares of the Shenandoah Valley, and her horse, a used John Deere. What about her language study, the Latin poets, the alternative life her father had set before her? A charade. She could admit it. Her mother had been right about that much.

Grace wasn't sure why she gave her father the news about Tommer first, though in one way it would be more interesting to him, more sociologically significant. These conversions, he explained, were generally abrupt and usually permanent. She was suddenly tired of her father's predictability, his tedious analyses. He was going on about the comfort she could take from this whole class of converts. That despite their perversion of school texts and the undue noise they made in the political process, these reborns were some of the safest citizens. Didn't drink and drive, didn't scatter venereal problems, carried their share of the tax load, and though they might be abrasive about an embryo's right to full-term, they were otherwise respectful, even protective, of freedom and property.

"Daddy, I'm going to marry Jerry Rice."

He grunted. "How long has he been back?"

"A few hours."

He kissed and congratulated her, and told her it was going to be hard on her mother. "She thought your Jerry was finished. Who's going to tell her she was wrong?"

Grace had her own way of spreading the word. She called her cousin Michael in Charlottesville. He wasn't there, but Starblanket took the message: an off-white affair in the Stilson Methodist Church, then the everybody-welcome in the barn. "Actually," Grace said, "not even off-white, to be honest." What she had in mind was a long, blue-and-ruby dress of Indian cotton that always had to be padded some to stay up.

They'd be there, Star promised. Would the band be hot?

The informal announcement was passed along to Aunt Michael, and from her to other Masons, and Grace's father switched the answering machine to record/monitor, not wishing to take part in the debate he knew was coming. As he said, "In a family full of independent millionaires nobody's boss."

Meanwhile, Grace was getting used to travelling in Jerry's old pickup, never cleaned or waxed, though the engine was dependable and quiet, like Jerry himself, she thought, a smooth performer, without show. A couple of nights after the proposal, Jerry brought Grace home for a change of clothes and some more overnight things. She came out of the house with a cassette, something she could play for him on the tape deck, driving back to his place.

"Waylon?" He doesn't like Waylon. He's not like that.

Not Waylon. "Family-incoming," she called it.

Jerry hadn't heard of them.

"No, you wouldn't have. It'll be mostly female." She hadn't had a chance to listen to the whole thing yet.

"Vocals?"

"Yes."

She slid the tape into its slot. There was a beep and the

hard voice of her Aunt Michael. "Eddie, it's your sister. Call when you can. Soon. A good-bye click, pause, and another tone. "Daddy, Georgia. This is a jolt about Gracie. We're all thinking about her and wondering. Why didn't she tell us? Why do we have to hear about it from Aunt Michael?"

The distant click, another beep, and Aunt Michael again. "Eddie, I called an hour ago. Sorry to be a plague. Don't let any invitations go out before we have a chance to talk. I want you to call me."

A disconnect, double beep, and an operator's repeated please-hang-up, which meant someone had refused to leave a message. Then Ailene asking Eddie please to call that evening, followed by a woman from the power-company billing office with a sugary threat. And Annalee calling Grace: "Nobody can get through to you two. Why don't you answer the phone?"

"Why don't you?" Jerry asked her.

"I've been hanging out with you all weekend."

He reached over and tugged at her thigh, and she slid closer, nestling against his shoulder. Her reformed, softer Jerry, dressed in corduroy and brushed leather brogans from Taiwan. Her man dressed neater than she did. He was looking slightly cow-eyed now, a little dopey with sexual satiation. He needed a nap.

"This is like reading your father's mail," Jerry said.

Aunt Michael again: "Eddie, I know you're right there listening to this. I've been told you never leave your study. . . . All right, I'll say my piece to your machine. Wait, it's six o'clock Sunday evening. I've called three times. Eddie, I'm only Grace's aunt, but I smell something wrong."

Jerry turned to sniff Grace's hair. She smirked and pushed at his chin until his eyes were on the road again. She thought it was time to stop the tape, but Jerry wanted to hear the rest. Aunt Michael had grown testy. "I don't know this man, but you know your local lore. The people up there could never be trusted, and now they're all waving the Confederate flag, trying to rewrite family history."

Maybe realizing she'd gone too far out on a dead limb, she told him, "Never mind. Do you know what the implications of a fall wedding are? A hurry-up job, that's what. An emergency situation. Grace might want to consider that. Oh, Eddie, you know Ailene has always imagined a proper reception for Grace down here in the hotel. In the ballroom. Even if it means bringing one of those wonderful colored bands down from Baltimore. The one you had at your wedding has shrivelled to two or three pieces. Remember that balloon-cheeked man who played trumpet and used to sing "They Cut Down the Old Pine Tree" at everyone's graduation?

"Look, anything appropriate can't possibly be arranged in one month. Eddie, I'll tell you honestly, I'm calling because Ailene asked me to. She says Grace has gotten to be just a smart aleck with her since you started her on the Latin, where she doesn't think for herself anymore, and you're to blame. Yes you are, Eddie. How could you think of having people there for a reception? Michael told me what it looks like, so overgrown you can't see a thing from the road. Like something lost in the jungle, you'd have to fly over in an airplane to spot it, and I don't blame the neighbors one bit. If you . . ." She'd had her three minutes. The machine cut her off.

"Who is that? One of the ones who's going to like me when she gets to know me?"

"I told you. My father's sister. Michael's mother. Daddy calls her the last fallen Daughter of the Confederacy. A cartoon."

"But she sounds real."

"The point is, to fall you'd have to start at some higher elevation."

Another beep and Aunt Michael was with them again: "Eddie, it is so rude of you to leave me talking into a box. Won't you speak to your sister? . . . So you won't, you're going to let me talk to silicone. . . ."

"Silicon. Silicon chips." Grace's father must have picked up the phone for a moment. Cut off, Aunt Michael rang again.

"Eddie, was that you?" She was denouncing Michael this time, the life he'd chosen in Charlottesville, still bumming around the university in one disguise and another, pretending to be a student with the dilettante slut, one of this new type with every scheme for making money except work. "It goes back to you, Eddie, to those summers Michael spent with you. Well, let's not look back. Let's just try to help the children into sensible futures. No wedding there until next spring is the best advice I can give you. By then, who knows? I'm hanging up now, Eddie."

Grace's mother came next with another plea to call and let her know exactly what was planned so far. She wasn't fighting the idea of the wedding now, only the style as she imagined it developing. "Really, dear, not that kind of dancing where the women get passed from one man to the next." Square dancing, she said, was for socially impoverished states like Vermont where you had to share what was available or go without. "Who's going to marry you? Do you want some help with the dress? Do you want Grandma Mason's veil? You can't leave us out of this, Grace."

Then they were listening to Jerry's parents. To his mother, with his father close by, interrupting. "Mr. Mason, this is Mrs. Rice, Jerry's mother. We couldn't get through to you, so I'm saying this after the beep. . . . He knows it's after the beep. . . . Excuse us. . . . Well, this is such a surprise about Jerry and your Grace. . . . Doesn't surprise me. . . . Gerald, will you be quiet . . . . Our pastor would like to meet with you and Grace. . . . Not him, just the girl. . . . Gerald! Just to get to know you. Would you call us?"

Grace called her mother and sisters that week and laid the thing out. Wedding date, October 14. The night before that, a dinner at the farmhouse for the two families. If hers couldn't offer blessings or congratulations, they should stay away.

"Of course you have my blessing," her mother told her. But how could they have the dinner at the farmhouse, which was overgrown with vines and barely furnished? Plus, no adequate china or silverware. Why not let Mrs. Rice have the dinner?

"Much too shy. It wouldn't even occur to her. Besides, it's something Daddy and I want to do." The chef and sous chef from the inn in the village, whose sons had once been devoted haymakers in Grace's fields, were providing the meal as their wedding present. They promised lobster, chocolate souffle, and several wines.

"Grace, what is the minister's name?"

"I told you, Reverend Shaplin."

"Is he a nice man, dear?"

"Of course. I mean, I hardly know him."

In fact, the service itself troubled Grace more than any other aspect of the coming celebration. The Reverend Elix Shaplin was a short, stolid man whose thin smile was more apt to flicker at a moral than a joke. He'd done nothing to put Grace at her ease at their first meeting, and made it clear he wasn't pleased to be marrying the couple, of whom neither belonged to his church. It was a favor to Jerry's parents, who themselves were irregular congregants and insignificant contributors to his offertory.

His rules were clear. "I don't allow people to write their own vows. I advise those who want to marry themselves to find another forum." His only flexibility was single or double ring. "So, you have a date?"

"The fourteenth of October," they said in unison. Fourteen, Jerry explained. The last two digits on each of their social security cards, and the lucky number of gallons, on the dot, he always pumps into his pickup. Mentioned only to lighten the moment, but Reverend Shaplin had seized the opportunity to comment on the modern confusion of superstition and faith. Grace stood silent, satisfied that for his fee, the unpleasant man would marry them.

Before they left, he wanted to show them something. Outside, high on the wall of his church, was the masonry outline of a pointed archway. There had once been a window there of unusual subtlety. "A beautiful stained-glass image of Noah and a dove over a turquoise sea. It was given to the church in 1935 by the Klan."

After protest fifteen years later, the stone had been laid up to obliterate it. On the inside of the church could be seen the faint outline of replastering in the same shape. "I show this to all people of no specific faith who ask a service of the church.

"And do you know what? Someone had the sense to leave the window. It's still up there between the walls. Waiting through the years for stone and plaster to be torn away. For sunlight to reawaken the glorious color. Perhaps in the next century. The church has the patience of millennia. It suffers the sin and passion of the moment without harm to itself. The window will be there when the Klan is as ancient a curiosity as your marriage."

Shaplin dismissed them with a question. "Do you understand what I've told you? I suspect you think you're getting away with something here. No. The church, without cynicism, can absorb a wanton act and give it dignity. Now, do you want to go on with this?"

Why should she let this man marry her? Jerry held firm. "My mother wants it here, we'll have it here."

The approaching wedding was moving her family into a calm of lowered voices and shared trouble. As if a tragedy had been scheduled for which there was no remedy but sympathy and support, for the bride and for one another. Only Michael and Star were effusive in their well-wishing. Still poaching in Charlottesville, and only occasionally employed, they were easily lured to the next adventure, and when Grace said "come as soon as you can," they took her at her word, arriving a full week before the wedding, settling in for a comfortable stay of free room and board. She put them in the downstairs guest room, which would hold the memory of naïve sport for Michael. Not to tease an old bruise, but to save the upstairs rooms for the former occupants, her mother and sisters; to reinhabit the house in the old, familiar pattern.

Jerry was keeping his distance in this last week of preparation. She understood. It was his sense of the seemly thing to do in the few days before their sleeping together was sanctioned by his mother's church. Grace was hanging around the house a lot, making sure the phone was answered and that her father received his messages. She'd hired two bands for the reception, one with a pedal steel that would satisfy Jerry and the local company and her own weakness for whiny close-harmony, and a conventional group who guaranteed themselves capable of a waltz and the whole Beatles canon, these for her sisters.

The heavy family-incoming continued, and this week it

was answered with live voices. Aunt Michael, on the trail of her wandering son, wanted to know where he had been put in the house. Eddie lied. "Michael and Star were shown to separate rooms." Where they moved after that was not his business.

Her mother, calling daily, said she was bringing up a few things to make the house more comfortable for the parties. Grace, she pointed out, might as well have hung a sign on herself years ago that said "FARM USE ONLY." "And we should have accepted it way back then. I know you're going to make a success of this."

"But Mum, I want you to be happy, too."

Grace was gladdened by the unexpected healing influence of the wedding, and the balm was spreading to her sisters, who even hinted they could have been persuaded to be bridesmaids. This thing her father kept saying, that they are all millionaires now, seemed so unimportant. There had been nothing until this wedding to begin spending her fortune on.

Starblanket was immediately fond of Eddie, attracted by the apparent scope of his knowledge and his disdain for the new suburbia around him. She seemed intrigued with the idea that this place, covered with nature's wild, green mess, and the surrounding manicured pastures, each settled with a showplace, had so recently been a game farm in the wilderness.

"You made a profit letting people come and shoot the ducks?"

"We certainly did. Grace was the flying instructor. Isn't that right, Michael?"

"She was more than that."

"Oh yes, she specialized in more than fowl husbandry."

Grace saw that this lustrous, reddish-blond woman was eager to get on with a week of surprises that might rival these allusions to a mischievous past in a free-thinking household. She saw Star immediately as searcher rather than settler, ready for flirtation with the next intellect that amused her. And her father was stepping right into the part.

"You know," he said, "it wasn't the hunters. Most of them were a decent sort. But brooding is an art, and incubation is a science. I just thought we should give the thing back to the birds. I wasn't going to be a voyeur anymore, peeping through shells at albumen to see if it had plans for bones and feathers."

"You have such a beautiful house. Michael told me all about the library. I hope there'll be time for you to show me through your shelves."

"A typical frame farmhouse built in the thirties," Eddie said. "With some gingerbread. A little leftover Victorian pretension. I doubt the library would interest you. Too dusty with classics."

"Oh no. I've monitored Virgil twice. I'm trying to get Michael to do Pindar and Greek Lyricism with me next semester. I mean, I don't know Greek, but I don't think you have to."

As they showed her around the house, the unused areas, bare walls, dusty beds, and vines climbing over the upstairs windows became a family humiliation to Grace, aggravated by Star's breezy appreciation.

"Oh, look at this! You could do so much with these rooms!"

Michael had grown into a sweet, but phlegmatic, young man, and Grace wondered how he had held on to this gadabout beauty whose conversation so frequently ignored him.

After the introductory tour Star had gone with Eddie into his library. Somehow she had brought the conversation around to the seventeen-year locust, which was not due for another thirteen, and its choice of a prime number. And Grace took Michael off for a look at the barn and what remained to be done to ready it for the wedding reception.

"God," he told her, "I don't know how many times she's recycled the stuff about the locusts."

Grace saw she had been fooled by his soft mouth and wounded eyes. He was capable of collusion. And ready with ideas for the barn.

"I don't know what to do with this," she said.

"That's easy. Push it into the center of the floor, open the doors, and turn it on. It'll keep people warm."

The incubator, the handsome cabinet of dark, polished oak, with the glass-covered dials circled in chrome, and brass hardware on the doors, was the kind of thing one of the Mason Hill immigrants would convert to a liquor-and-ice chest in a basement bar. "If you don't know what to do with something," Michael said, "you put it right in the middle of things. So people think it's essential."

She was thinking how much he sounded like her father, a self-assured master of irony, and just as likely to walk off to a lonely corner and be mysterious. He suggested hanging the four, large, stainless-steel hovers from overhead beams. They could be giant, reflecting lamp shades with their red heat lamps.

How quickly, she said, all the impedimenta that had worried her in the barn had become lux over her wedding ball. Baggage into light.

"Hunh?"

"I'm sorry. Daddy was pushing so hard on the Latin. Don't worry. I'll get over it." But what if she says something like that to Jerry?

She'd forgotten for a moment that Jerry was the one who lay ahead of her, covering her final retreat from her mother's hotel and her father's library. She thought how wise she'd been to have chosen his cunning simplicity. And how lucky, as an outsider, to be drawn in love into a native family with ties to the latter-day planters and dairymen. If there were fields to be turned, she and Jerry would find them.

They went back to the library where Eddie and Star had been making over each other's busy brains, flying from Wittgenstein's smart machine guns to the resurrection of Homer from a prose limbo of inferior translators to his place in the poetic pantheon, to the asymptote as metaphor for tragic human partnerships. Their hands were reaching out now and then, as if in these happy discoveries they might touch each other's wonderful ideas.

"Don't you hate it when they show off like that?" Michael veered away from entering the room, repelled by the wrong magnetic pole, went off through the hall and out the back door to be on his own, leaving Grace to listen to the two minds at exercise.

Grace had been thinking about which room her mother would use when she arrived Thursday evening. She could share her room, or Annalee's, since Annalee, divorced, would be coming alone. But should Grace lead her mother in some direction in the house by making up a bed ahead of time, and spare her and Eddie what might be an awkward moment? She thought yes, she would fix a cot in Annalee's room. Annalee, she supposed, would take that, and insist that her mother use the larger bed.

Georgia and her husband, still childless, could make themselves comfortable in Georgia's old room with the queen-size. Aunt Michael, like it or not, would have to settle for the attic quarters where her son had once slept. The thing out of balance in all this was that Eddie got the master bathroom to himself, while all the others upstairs would share the cramped toilet, sink, and shower stall down the hall.

With such distractions Grace avoided the thought of Reverend Shaplin, whose service loomed over her wedding day. While Eddie and Star amused each other that week with flashy nuggets of knowledge, Grace went off with Michael into the wild of her remaining acres. They sat by the river, and sometimes in the barn, chatting across the missing years.

She wanted him to know how right this was that she was marrying Jerry, wanted to make him truly believe it. It wasn't just a false test her family might apply, not just the usual trap of confusing knowledge with intelligence that bothered her. Together she and Jerry went beyond obvious infatuation, which of course was there, but not so important as their mutual pleasure in fields under grain and the big green machines. "I think we're going to surprise everyone. They're afraid it can't last. Or maybe afraid it will."

While they talked she sat leaning against Michael, and walking back through the undergrowth, she took his hand, letting him know she was not ashamed of their old intimacy, and that their continuing affection should be nothing to hide or fear. Their lives were on course now, parallel, and moving into safe harbors. Wasn't that the way he saw it?

He had pulled his hand free. Had both of them in his pockets for safekeeping. "If you mean, will Star and I get married, not likely."

"No?"

"She asked me. I said, no. I can't really trust her."

"She wanders?"

"Not like that. Not between beds. From mind to mind. From book to book. It's always the last idea she's touched, or the last person she's talked to."

Entering the house, they heard Star sprinkling laughter over one of Eddie's naughty poems.

7. FAMILY HANDS

Ailene had sent a list of names to Mrs. Rice, people from her Roanoke circle expecting invitations to the church service; people, Grace supposed, that her mother hoped would not trouble themselves with the long drive to an upcountry performance, but all the same, could be expected to pay tribute to their friend's daughter. And since Grace had failed to name a silver pattern, Aunt Michael had chosen one for her, registering it with several stores in Roanoke, then calling the information up to shops in Winchester, Leesburg, Middleburg, and Ripton Corner. As if a grand society stretching from the river out across the subdivisions and malls of Piedmont Virginia were anticipating her niece's wedding.

Grace and Jerry were handling the general invitation to the wedding ball with phone calls and a poster in the village café, asking all the people they could think of. They happily lost control of the party numbers. A crush of people would please Grace most. She'd put a sign up at the entrance to Mason Hills, welcoming the suing neighbors into her celebration. Her mother's groaning disapproval became another whimper of resignation.

And Thursday evening after dark, Ailene arrived with Annalee. Her new station wagon was stuffed with things coming back to the farmhouse. They had a large rental trailer in tow, the same kind Ailene had used when she left the farm. Their greetings were cordial, Grace thought, even the offering of a limp hand to Star. She watched her mother and father embrace warily.

"Hey!" Star said, "I've seen that station wagon in the

ads. That's twenty-five thousand. Not just transportation, hunh?"

Ailene asked Michael if he'd carry in some bags. "How do we get to the house?"

"This way," Eddie said, "through the chlorophyll arcade." He led them between ailanthus and locust saplings overhung with honeysuckle and wild grapevines.

Grace tried to whisper the sleeping arrangements to her mother.

"Absolutely not," Ailene cried out. "I'll sleep in the room where I've always slept." And there'd be no secret about it. First thing brought in from the trailer was the chaise longue that had always been in the master bedroom. She let everyone know this would be made up with her own sheets and blanket. She'd be damned if she'd share a bathroom with the rest of the household.

Annalee drew Grace away from the others. "Let them worry about where things go. You're going to tell me all about Jerry. Everything, you little sneak, we're so out of touch. God, isn't it strange to be so rich?"

Grace felt a rush of love for her sister. So much of Annalee's early kindness, her lovely eyes and mouth, had been spent on a marriage that soured her. It told in the way she twisted her face when she described the man who had never been satisfied with himself or her. Not in her little age lines masked by makeup, but in grimaces and contortions of irony for which there would never be cosmetic relief. And now she was at pains to give Grace warnings without spoiling her bliss.

The explanation of her terrible mistake, so lacking in details of personality, laughably simple, was nevertheless presented for comparison with Grace's romance. "I'd been spending so much time with him," Annalee said. "Then he left me miserable. When he asked me to marry him six months later I was delirious. I'd been a wet mess for all that time. And the pain went away. Of course I'd marry him. Why would I want to keep on being miserable? Tell me about Jerry?"

"You'll see." Grace knew the first impressions were going to be dirty fingernails and bad grammar, and all of her family were going to have to swallow hard and bite their tongues a few times before accepting Jerry in the fold. They'd be wowed by his usefulness as a master mechanic before they ever let him into the inner circle. He'd be under the hoods of their cars, sneaking up on their affections in a greasy shirt and oil-black hands.

"Grace, tell me this. Is he gentle or rough with you? Does he want to hold on all night in the summer, too, or just when it's cold?" Her little tests for marital success made her that much more pathetic. Grace reached out to run a hand through her sister's honey-blond hair, and Annalee gathered her in a desperate little embrace. "Gracie, what are we going to do with all the money?"

That night, before going up to her room, Grace noticed the old silverware in its velvet-lined chest had been carried into the dining room. And the Moran, the dark, mountain scene with crystal falls, had been rehung over its telltale, discolored place in the central hallway. More things were coming in, and she heard Ailene tell her father, "Eddie be careful with that. It all goes back after the wedding," her voice raised to reach through the house.

In the kitchen, four sets of china and the old crystal were already in familiar cabinets along with the platter that had held the Sunday feasts of her childhood, and a gilt-edged tureen that Grace knew had family provenance significant to her mother.

All through the house little watercolors, oils, and prints,

more loved for their familiarity than their quality, were re-
appearing over the light-colored patches that betrayed their
departure. It was a simple puzzle of missing rectangular
pieces, completed within minutes and bringing a warmth of
recognition and repletion that lifted Grace up to contented
sleep.

Her mother came to her room with a last question.
"Grace, have you done everything you want to do before the
rules change?"

"What rules?"

"The marriage rules." She kissed Grace on the forehead
and pulled up her covers.

When she came down in the morning, her mother had
Eddie and Michael at work again. Georgia and her husband,
Wendell, had arrived after midnight in a big van with more
furniture. They were sleeping in, while refurnishing of the
house continued. Her mother's cherished dozen ladder-backs
had been placed around the dining room table, and the four
hoop Windsors with sculpted seats, along with two side tables
and a walnut secretary, whose removal had left the living
room a bare theater with a single bench, were polished and in
position again.

Georgia came down to breakfast in pajamas and floppy
slippers, her hair all ajumble. Wendell was worn out, she said,
and still sleeping. She took Grace in her arms, and wished her
every happiness in the world. "Little Grace, I can't believe
you. Just swallowed the canary by the looks of you."

But it was Georgia who might have been bashful about
appearance, her eyes half-closed, lips puffy, chin rubbed
red, listing and bleary though well pleased, like an advertise-

ment for the pleasures of a marriage bed that travelled well.

Her Wendell had recently quit his job as a printer's salesman, a job requiring extra hours and too much travel, and which had barely supported their household. He'd never liked the work, only the advancements and providing for Georgia. What sense in that now, she reasoned, when they'd be making a hundred and fifty thousand, just in interest. "Who's going to manage yours, Grace?"

Actually, Georgia didn't want to talk about money. Her advice was not to have children for at least two years. "Give yourselves time." Her formula was, "For every major quarrel, add another six months to the waiting period." But childless herself, how could she know?

Neither children nor quarrels loomed in Grace's vision. She let her sister chatter on without revealing that Jerry's count was low. But why not have children if you could, she thought. Why not make it more difficult to argue? Why not engineer a family toward compromise? A farm, even in shrunken form, insisted on fertility. She would never be shamed away from that.

As the morning disappeared, and their home was made ready for hospitality, Ailene's worry turned to the out-of-doors. "Eddie, I want somebody to get out there and pull the weeds off this house."

"Go ahead, you can't hurt the wisteria."

Wendell appeared in the kitchen, bleary as Georgia before him. He was ready to give his weekend to being helpful, unlike Michael, who had wondered off on his own again.

With no time to cut back the overgrown yard, Ailene and Annalee decorated the passageway of vegetation between driveway and front porch with bright paper lanterns and wind chimes. Like bower birds building a tunnel of love, twittering with dismay and approval, they delighted Grace as she passed under their handiwork on her way to find her cousin.

Instead of Michael, she found her father and Star walking quietly up from the river.

"He went that way," Star said. "Maybe you can solve his mood."

Grace learned later that Michael had taken someone's rowboat and drifted several miles downriver to another landing, then moseyed back up the river road, taking his own good time, stopping at a vegetable stand where he made himself a tomato sandwich, all to avoid his mother's arrival. She was already soaking her indignation in a hot bath when he got back.

Michael was ready to defy her command to move out of the girl's room. Let tears fall. The problem wouldn't go away. Star's things were taken to Annalee's room where she could sleep on the cot that had been set up for Ailene.

The caterers came at five, and the household switched focus from room assignments to the dinner party. There had to be place cards, Aunt Michael insisted. Star made the seating plan into a mathematical teaser in which there were two givens—Eddie and Ailene at either end of the table—and ten unknowns, some of which she called incompatible integers and some too chummy to be placed together. Certainly bride and groom must be separated, and herself from Michael. And Georgia from Wendell.

"Leave her alone," Ailene told Grace. "She seems to have a good head for it."

Star dared Eddie to calculate the number of possible arrangements given the restrictions she'd mentioned, and now they had their heads happy at play again with pad and pencil. A few minutes later Star had abandoned the math and produced the social solution:

Ailene

Mr. Rice	Wendell
Grace	Annalee
Michael	Jerry
Georgia	Aunt Michael
Star	Mrs. Rice

Eddie

"It's your party. What do you think?"

Grace saw that she'd be convenient to Michael's protective arm, with an easy angle to Jerry's eyes. Star had put herself next to Eddie with no damage to essential protocol. Mr. and Mrs. Rice, guests of honor, could still be on the right hands of her mother and father. Annalee and Ailene would share Wendell's gracious manners. And Aunt Michael, though she'd complain, would be secretly pleased for the opportunity to vet the groom and his mother.

It was noticed that Eddie would have four women at his end. A chance to play the peacock, Ailene observed, though more likely, Grace supposed, he'd fade away into one of his mysterious silences. No matter, Star would be there to take up the slack. Yes, Grace thought, there was something in the arrangement for everyone. But as the dinner hour came closer, she was forced at last to imagine the Rices actually sitting captive among her family.

Aunt Michael began the evening on her very best behavior. She did not whisper that the Rices' suits were shiny or that Mrs. Rice's hairdresser had overdone it with the rinse.

Grace heard her tell Mr. Rice, "My brother's black pajamas are actually formal wear in Southeast Asia." Inventing, apologizing, she was playing healer to the ceremony. She took it on herself to show all the Rices through the house before dinner, stopping now and then for the lineage of a piece of furniture.

She made too much fuss under the Moran, and Jerry remarked that from his angle the whole thing looked like varnish on top of creosote. "To tell you the truth," Aunt Michael told him, "I've never cared for it myself, but Ailene is a bit of a fool for this one."

"No, no," Mrs. Rice said. "Very impressive, I'm sure."

Her husband rebuked her for being silly and impressionable. Grace understood. There was nothing in this house he could not have in his own if he took his wallet to the right auctions. Jerry asked her what was going on. "A lot of this stuff wasn't here last week."

Ailene rang the little silver dinner bell, never in Grace's memory used to call people to a meal. It had been a curiosity of her childhood along with the rest of the sterling in an off-limits cabinet, and only rung surreptitiously by her and her sisters to make sure it still had a sound. Now its tinkling gave a genteel formality to the dinner call, and in the golden glow of the dining room under candlelight Grace worried again for her guests.

It was quite extraordinary the way the polished oak table shone under the tall silver candlesticks, and the crystal goblets and blue china caught the wavering light. Georgia and Annalee had done the centerpiece, a masterful wildflower burst of blue and ruby, as if they had forgiven and blessed the colors of her wedding dress.

Jerry stood at the chair next to her until Star showed him his mistake. All of them except Eddie walked around the table looking for their names, surprised and delighted to discover their dinner partners, even Jerry, who seemed relieved of a duty.

Grace had counted on the lobsters to get elbows into action and force people to talk about the food if nothing else. Someone would surely claim ignorance of how to enter the shell and how to proceed once inside. Grace had imagined Jerry's mother in the part of innocent. Instead, Mrs. Rice said she and Gerald went once a month to a lobster night in Manassas. She was expert at lip suction on the swimmers and not a bit squeamish about the mustard.

Aunt Michael was the one who cried for help, and Jerry seized the moment. "I always start this way," he said. He tore a large claw from the body, held it in his palm and smacked it hard with the heavy end of his knife, sending a salt spray in Annalee's direction.

"Oh, would you do that for me?" Aunt Michael begged.

"Jerry, dear," his mother said, "why don't you use the tool in front of you?"

He was doing it his way again, this time showering himself.

"Oh, look!" Aunt Michael had seen that the droplets were not absorbed by his jacket but sat up like water on a waxed car. There was laughter and approval all around, overriding Mrs. Rice's gentle scolding. Nothing was said for the moment about the bruises under the monogram on the sterling handle.

Star said the lobsters were making her think of the natural selection of exoskeletal organisms. Michael's chin fell a bit and Grace put a secret hand on his knee. No one, not even Eddie, was encouraging Star in this difficult direction. In her bright way, Star was explaining how soft the university was in invertebrate biology. Mrs. Rice, across from her, was nodding politely.

The wine was brought in and poured after presentation

of a bottle at each end of the table. A well-regarded Virginia Zinfandel, the caterers announced. Mrs. Rice allowed that, blindfolded, she couldn't tell one wine from another. "You're absolutely right," Eddie told her. "I couldn't either."

"What kind of grape is it?" Annalee asked.

"Zinfandel," Mr. Rice reminded her.

"No," Annalee said. "I mean the name of the grape."

"That is the name of the grape," Mr. Rice said. "Zinfandel."

Stricken and blushing, Annalee was absolved by Mr. Rice's promise that he had once made the very same blunder, and that the wine business, after all, was as much the cultivation of a market as a grape. "It could as well be a brand name."

His indulgence for Annalee struck a warm note, kindling good will around the table, and conversation came more easily.

"I can't stand it anymore," Aunt Michael said brightly, and she reached over with her napkin to wipe away the liquid beads that still stood up on Jerry's jacket. "This must be one of the fabrics invented by the Delaware people. You're so clever to wear it for lobster."

"And can I do something for you?" Jerry asked her.

"Of course, dear."

He took a chicory flower from the centerpiece and placed it carefully next to a streak of gray in Aunt Michael's flipped hair.

"This is such a charmer." She took his arm affectionately. "He's been telling me why the Buick coughs in the morning."

Mr. Rice leaned in front of Grace to ask Michael, "What's your line of work?"

A little panic circled the table, a concern for Michael's uncomfortable silence, and Grace wished she could tell them all her cousin had done, everywhere he'd been, all he was capable of. Why should he have to explain that this year he was working as a university messenger, while he continued his informal education, reading and poaching?

His lips were finally moving when Mr. Rice gently withdrew his question. "It's really none of my business." He'd been thinking so much, he said, about the problem young people have choosing careers, balancing ideals with reality.

"Michael," Grace told them proudly, "is going to make a million," then halted in a confusion of her own. Now the silence was hers to fill. People were waiting. The incredible truth was that eight of them were already millionaires—herself, her sisters, her mother and father, Mr. and Mrs. Rice, whose business, she knew, was worth far more than that, and Jerry, in time. No, she thought, Jerry tomorrow. In this company what could her boast for Michael be taken for but inept condescension.

Her hand went stealthily to his knee again. Her cousin, she said, was already a wise man. He had studied natural medicine in the Southwest. This, too, was a mistake. The hippie history would be as quickly despised here as mere wealth.

Perhaps if she could begin with the right detail. "In California a bird made some of his hair into a nest." With that she was hopelessly lost, but Mrs. Rice called up from her end.

"Yes, I've seen that with the hair from horses' tails."

Michael began to tell about the nest and its curse on his life. He went through it slowly and precisely with remarkable ease. They put down their lobster tools and listened. Grace saw that Star had turned away from her father to be amused again by a story she must have heard a dozen times or more.

"All those chicken carcasses suffering for me." He made them laugh, then wait, and laugh again. This was his gift, his charm, and Grace relaxed as he entertained them all. He held the table that way for at least five minutes as deserts were crossed, tires went flat, and, at last, tetracycline was swallowed.

The hair woven around the nest. His thinking doubling back on itself. His life going round and round, coming out at the beginning. The medicine man's prediction that he'd never get anywhere. He explained his serious circles with a doubtful distance that made them all the more significant.

Mrs. Rice said it was wonderful he was back on his feet. Georgia thought it was a beautiful story that only lacked the proper ending.

"That's why it's beautiful," Star said, almost too quietly to be heard.

Annalee wondered aloud if Michael had used the funny mushrooms.

Yes, they were in the Indian's drugstore, though not frequently prescribed.

Jerry led them all back to work on the lobsters. He was paying Grace almost no attention. For him she could have been wrapped in brown paper, not to be opened until tomorrow night when no one was looking.

Michael was just getting to mouse bones and the hair that got away, but Grace was distracted by something Mr. Rice was telling her mother. "Custom farming? A nice idea, but it won't work for them. It's not practical to move the large machines more than ten miles." He was twirling his wine glass by the stem, and her mother's hand shot forward to cover his wrist.

"Really?"

"Yes." And I'll tell you a dealer's little secret. It's been gentleman farmers around here, and more machines than the land needs. It's a kind of vanity. Having your own."

"I see," her mother said. "If Grace goes too far, she'll just run into someone else's territory."

Grace had to strain to hear the rest because Mr. Rice was

lowering his voice to fit the shame of what he was telling her mother. "I have a used sixty-thousand-dollar machine on my lot that won't bring three thousand at auction."

Across the way she saw Aunt Michael take Jerry's arm again, drawing him back into conversation. And a moment later her father was reaching over to pat Mrs. Rice's shoulder, dismissing her apology for not doing enough for these celebrations. All around Grace, this unexpected laying on of family hands.

The chocolate soufflé was carried in, fallen before its time and a little soggy. Aunt Michael giggled like a naughty child, and could not stop, even for Ailene's explanation that forgave the chef and blamed her own long-winded conversation. Later, Grace discovered what Jerry had whispered to set off her aunt: if the girl sitting across from his mother kept gassing at the same speed, she might repump the desert.

8. DEARLY BELOVED

"Gracie, they are all so genuine! Especially his father!"

The Rices were gone and there was a gathering in the living room where post-dinner impressions flew with good cheer from all quarters. Her family seemed suddenly happy with the prospect of upcountry in-laws for Grace.

Aunt Michael had a private apology. "I thought you might have a seven-month surprise in there," tapping Grace's rigid belly with the back of her hand. "Listen dear, your boy is going to be fine. Promise me one thing. When you have children, you'll get their teeth straightened. I know some people think a gap in front is attractive, but it's no substitute for a pretty mouth like yours. His mother was so quiet, poor thing. I liked her, I really did.

Annalee thought Jerry's laid-back way, his refusal to match all the Mason airs, was just what the family needed. "I told him I'm looking for nephews and nieces."

Georgia, who had been in a lively chat with her mother about Mr. Rice's great common sense, turned to wave an admonishing finger at the idea of making babies too soon, before a sensible trial period. Strange, Grace thought, that her sister should have to compensate this way for her own barren marriage.

"From what I've heard," Star said quietly, but not quietly enough, "they've already had their trial. Now it's off to happy prison." She had her arms wrapped around Michael, and her cheek against his, as if what she'd observed was their shared wisdom on Grace and her marriage. He seemed content for the moment with his gypsy scholar.

For Grace's family this was, after apology and reappraisal, still a matter of breeding between two orders of life, an interracial marriage. The boy with small hands and stubby fingers, short-waisted, and vision foreshortened by the chain link around his father's acre of machines. Voice a little high. Admit it, a runty sort of breed for all its folk wisdom.

And long, lithe Grace, a mutant only in behavior, from a family that could tie itself in stubborn knots to Rolfes and Carters through two grandmothers to whom credit was given for long backbones and noses that followed a straight line out of wise foreheads. This marriage was seen as something that could be turned in a better direction with an orthodontist's wire and some dominant Mason genes. They'd favor a lengthened backbone and a little more space between the eyes.

The family didn't know that Grace and Jerry had just argued. Whispering at the door. "What did your father mean we'd never make it farming?"

"He likes to be the prophet."

"We are going to use the machines?"

"We can try. See how it goes."

"No, this was definite. This was our work."

"Work? Grace, you don't have to work. You never had to work."

"What have I been doing here since I was fifteen?" The others had begun to gather around them and she pulled Jerry out the door and through the bower, under wind chimes tinkling stupidly. She demanded an answer.

"No one in your family works," he said.

Thank God she hadn't said my cousin happens to be a messenger for the university. Or, a man is talking to my father about publishing some of his translations.

"Me! I work!"

"Yes, you do, Grace. I'm sorry, you do work."

His apology seemed both heartfelt and false. For Jerry, too, it was a matter of breeding. She could never outgrow the deformity, call it a birth defect if you like. It wasn't that no Mason had ever pulled the trigger on a deer, or a dove. Or that most of their land had been traded away and thus there was no longer a way to prove themselves equal to the land. In his mind it was still this: Rices worked because they always had to. Masons worked although they never had to.

"Your family's loaded," she said. It could only bounce off because Rices wore clothes, faces, hands to prove who they were and who they'd been. They were never going to let money show. They were just storing it up while they went about in the local disguise, overalls.

"What do you want? Why are we doing this?"

"You remember," he said backing her gently up against the door of his truck, "you were going to show me all those new ways to make children. Starting tomorrow night." He kissed her on the forehead the way he might have pecked at a sister, said good-bye, and followed his parents' car down the driveway. What he wanted most was a family? So much he'd be willing to start with a partner not quite worthy?

What was attracting her now? Why so determined to go through with this? She considered the bold fluctuation of her desire, and his new fervor, which might have more to do with time elapsed between love-makings than any maturation of spirit.

She desired him. Liked to stare at his face, liked the way his fingers gripped a spoon, the way he said her name at the beginning and end of a question: "Grace, will you show me another way to make a family, Grace?" Desire was its own argument. If she liked these insignificant things, she must like something larger, something that needn't be named. She watched his truck's taillight trace his last retreat from her bed.

They must have been waiting to see who'd be last to retire, how the house would settle itself for the evening. Ailene once more to her chaise longue in Eddie's room? Star to the cot next to Annalee again, as she'd promised? Aunt Michael could yawn all she pleased; Star was debating the culture of a northern Virginia underclass.

"I'm not talking about the Rices," she said. This was about the few whites in the near country who were still tenants, stable hands, kitchen help. Hadn't she seen them all around her in Carlin, where they ran up unmanageable bills at a jot-em-down store?

"No," Eddie said, "they have no culture. They don't even know the names of the trees."

"Oh yes," Star insisted, all around there were hints of a racial memory, Anglo-Saxon speech patterns. In a couple of months they would show their mid-winter stirrings for restorative ceremony transcending their television-taught Christmas.

"Speech pattern, bull."

"Who said that?"

Annalee had said it, and Grace loved her for it, but Star was already offering her example. "Aye, I saw the common critter, the long-haired bastard, rising naked in the morning to shake his lousy blankets."

"Who was that?" "Nobody talks that way."

Yes, her neighbor had said precisely that. It was the day after Michael spent his first night in Carlin.

"They look through your windows?" Aunt Michael asked.

"We were sleeping on the porch," Star said proudly.

Grace had wanted to dismiss Star as the simple foil of her father and a false chapter in Michael's education, but the girl had outfaced all the family names for her: gypsy scholar, little insurance whore, Michael's latest. More likely, Michael's only. None of them could stop her in argument.

A marvel in short takes of knowledge, she seemed untroubled by the occasional lapse in Michael's attention. It was Grace's comfort to think of her now as an insentient model, perfectly prepared in face, dress, and intellect, and quite stiff in bed, probably a complainer about each slightly pulled hair, balking at every little broken rule of hygiene. It was Grace's secret notion that she alone in the household could have made Michael happy with a complete sexual freedom.

Her reverie was interrupted by Georgia remarking again on their perfect sense of timing in letting the place go. Grace supposed this had to do with the moment of her perceived failure on the land. Star told her no, she had it from Michael by way of Annalee, that it would have been sold much sooner, and at a far lower price if Ailene hadn't realized Annalee's marriage was failing. They had only waited until the divorce settlement was final, in case the departing husband should make a claim on her share of the estate. By this lucky delay they had not only saved her money but found the top of the market. "What are you going to do with yours?"

"I'm going to bed with it."

"Going up already, dear?" Her mother was beside her with news. "I wanted it to be a surprise. The furniture and things are staying here." It was like an offering of flesh and spirit more than wood and canvas. "It belongs here. A lot of it was in storage anyway. I didn't have room for it in my little box of a townhouse. It's for all of you children." She didn't mention Eddie though he was the one who'd be living here with it.

Grace climbed the stairs and looked back at all of them watching her retreat. She felt that in some backhanded way her mother was healing the house for something more than the wedding. The others were bubbling about the permanent return of the furnishings. All except Michael, who slipped into the hall and out the front door, signal of another mood. This time Star went after him.

Georgia followed Grace up the steps and into her room. "You're not fooled by Michael and the girl, are you?" giving Grace no time to answer. "Michael's nice but the two of them are such a confidence team." They were playing on his desert mysteries and Star's wandering scholarship. "They're the ones without money here." It was like selling their lives, Georgia said, telling and retelling for a meal and a bed until one day they'd have it in shape for typing.

Really, couldn't Grace see it was a spiritual canard, the idea that Michael could have been doomed to turn in circles by a hair-thieving bird and an Indian prophet. Just a story that could soften a heart, be told anywhere for a bed and breakfast.

Also Michael's excuse for the indolence that had taken over his life.

"But he's here again," Grace argued, "right back where he began with nothing to show for it."

"He's got the girl to show for it."

Georgia and the others could think of his life as a self-fulfilling prophecy if they liked. Grace preferred the idea of a vague, unpremeditated circle that had brought him back to the game farm.

To steady her nerve in church, Grace looked up at the dark shape of the missing window while she waited for the musical cue and her father's arm. Jerry already stood at the altar with Reverend Shaplin. Mr. Rice was just behind them with the ring. No best man, no maid of honor. The minimal ceremony she and Jerry had agreed on.

The timing was thrown off by her mother's late arrival. Ailene was having her orchid repinned, but Annalee and the two women still had to be escorted to the front before the dominant vibration of the organ could create a pace for Grace's nervous legs. She could see Shaplin staring over his glasses, down the aisle, and Jerry was stepping in place as if he wished the marble font next to him were a urinal.

"How much patience does the church have now?" she asked scarcely under her breath. She knew there was loss for herself in her scorn, that it diminished her wedding day, but she discounted this by congratulating herself on how empty the church was, how few would witness Shaplin's perfunctory act. It put him in his place as just a legal stamp on a properly private matter.

There were only her own family and Jerry's and two men in dark, square-shouldered suits, sitting halfway down the aisle on the groom's side. Either uninvited or Jerry had asked them at the last minute and forgotten to mention it to her. The one sat tall and stiff, his red tie showing a broad swathe under his jutting collar; the old man, slumped and rumpled. Grace knew but could not quite credit that they were Tommer and his father come to honor the wedding with their new religion. By the time she started down the aisle there was no doubt of it.

She was walking too fast. Twice her father pulled back on her arm to slow her. She carried no flowers because there'd be no one to take them from her when the ring was placed on her finger. "Don't try one of those pull tops," Shaplin had warned them, "or there'll be no wedding," again as if it had only been in their minds to mock his church. It had happened to him—a couple using an aluminum ring from a soda can.

Grace passed her mother and aunt, one in pink, the other in light-blue silk, more bridal than herself. Handed up to the altar, she was beside Jerry at last.

"Dearly beloved." Grace felt her hands sliding down the back of her dress in search of pockets.

"Dearly beloved." An appropriate way to start, she thought, though not really what she would call Jerry, or quite the way she felt about him, and why was Shaplin repeating himself.

"Dearly beloved." This time Grace saw that the minister was distracted by a movement in his church. Looking over her shoulder she saw Tommer and his father advancing. Now that the event was under way they were coming forward, row by vacant row, improving on inferior tickets.

"We are gathered together here in the sight of God, and in the presence of mine enemies. . . ." Shaplin stopped, stricken with his blunder, shunted off the marriage track into the familiar psalm. Slowly he brought his words back into line.

"Surely the cup runneth over when man and woman are joined."

He left the mangled text for a moment to lecture from the heart. Grace assumed there was some logic passing over her head, too amazed by what was happening to her to make sense of it. There was "the mystical union between Christ and his Church," not to be confused, Shaplin declared, with the union now taking place between this man and this woman, for which the rules were abundantly clear, and from which there could be no backsliding.

Why "not to be confused with," Grace wondered. This was in fact a most mysterious union, the one between her and Jerry. She heard "reverently, discreetly, and in the fear of God." She was watching Jerry, who seemed to be in awe of the words themselves. For him, Grace supposed, each one could have been a brick placed on his shoulders, each separately important. In no time he might become a willing hod carrier to the church's dogma.

"Let them speak now, or else hereafter forever hold their peace."

Shaplin was fully composed again. His challenge rang against the stone walls of his nearly empty church, and the thin, piping voice answering the echo seemed ludicrous. "I can't hold it. I've got to say it."

"Family?" Shaplin asked Jerry.

"No, no one told them to come."

Tommer's father had risen, wild-eyed and shaky, to tell them troubling things that condemned and ought to prevent this marriage.

Shaplin stopped him, and Tommer shot up beside his father. "You asked," he said, pointing at the minister. "Let him speak like the book says."

"The book says no such thing. You're trespassing here."

"Those who trespass against us," the old man agreed.

Tommer turned to Jerry's family as if they were going to be his fair jury. "There's a sign in front. What do the white letters say? They say 'ALL ARE WELCOME.' Now let him speak."

"That's Sundays."

But the man knew his rights. He could not hold his peace. He began with the color of the tarpaulin he'd stolen from the Masons, black and greasy as the hair of the fornicator who was asking to be their son-in-law.

Shaplin told Jerry, "Stay where you are. We'll wait till he's finished."

"He'll forgive what's been done, and that's plenty. Not what's still being planned."

Grace was suddenly interested in what he might have to say. She saw her Aunt Michael nodding agreement, like the porcelain doll she'd brought as a wedding present, her head set to bobbing by the latest prodding.

"He's going to cheat, I'll guarantee."

Mr. Rice reached his side, and Tommer's father allowed himself to be led away. In the aisle he turned back with a prediction of their damnation. "And he'll cut that place back. Make it grass like it's supposed to be."

Tommer was still there, demanding a turn not to hold his peace. Jerry had jumped down and was heading for him, but the two families got in his way. Shaplin was telling Grace, "That's all, you'll have to find somewhere else."

Tommer was backing down the aisle. The door opened behind him and his father popped his head in again. "You join them, and they'll fly asunder."

The stretch limo hired by Jerry's father against Grace's wishes took them into Chamberton, but the justice of the peace wasn't home. Jerry popped the complimentary champagne, and clicked on the TV over the jump seat. The sharpest image reaching the screen looked like a man made of vibrating rice, whose voice promoted a car from Japan.

Take us to Worton, Jerry ordered. There they found the J.P.'s rules inflexible. No same-day weddings. "You want me to do it, make an appointment a week ahead." If they couldn't wait, there was a man bonded for the job over the ridge in Berryville. For a hundred dollars he'd do an instant service.

Would next week be soon enough? Jerry asked her.

She supposed so. They got back into the long car and pointed the driver toward Mason Hills where the party would be waiting for them. Jerry removed his coat and tie, and loosened his collar. He pulled down all the window shades, then the screen between them and the driver. Solemn, as if searching her eyes for complicity. "There," he said, "now it's dark enough to see the television."

"We could just tell everyone we're married. That way they can all enjoy the party. No," Jerry thought better of his own suggestion. "Let's tell the truth."

Grace urged more speed out of the chauffeur. She turned off the television and moved herself between Jerry and the screen. "You know," he said, "if Shaplin had wanted to he could have just said, 'you're married.' That would have done it. If you want to blame someone, blame him."

Grace didn't want to blame anyone. Not resentful, she was looking forward only to the party in the barn where the two bands were waiting. Delivered by the odd miracle of Tommer's wretched faith, she could approach the evening as a secret quantity, still unattached and ready to flirt in any direction. The man sitting next to her might even have a chance, though he was being such a boor with the television.

The change hardly surprised her; it seemed so slight.

Like ice, as Star had explained her altered states with Michael. One minute, solid. The change of a single degree, and before you knew it, meltdown and a serious run-off of affection.

"I'm fluid!" Grace shouted insanely. But no one heard her because she was shouting to herself.

She put up her shade and hit the window button. They were coming through the gap over the ridge. The setting sun made orange lightbursts in the distant windows of Mason Hills. Her own house and barn, covered with green and higher than the new homes, looked like bushes shaped by topiary whim into country architecture.

"What are we going to do with that place, anyway?"

"Nothing," she said. "We're not going to do anything with it."

"Nothing?"

"We tried everything. Now we're trying nothing. What farmers do in the winter. Only we're doing it all year 'round."

"Like always?"

"The land is real!" Grace was screaming to herself again. "And we're proving it." If he couldn't see that, he was blind.

Her wedding became more remote. All Jerry's "we's" were now presumptuous. To be single was to be ready for any happy accident. Not just a freedom to wander after a new lover, but to control, alone, the use of the last strange piece of land her family held, the square frying pan, whose most valuable use had become neglect. The farm was wildly germinating. And the more wild it became, the more it irritated the community, and the higher their offerings. The neighbors had lost in court, and two of them had come with softer voices and credit references, also a builder with a scheme for a zoning waiver to accommodate river-view condominiums.

Grace had sent them away. She was holding out for an agricultural miracle, a yet-to-be-revealed secret of intensive gardening that could transform seven acres into seven hundred, and set her again over the lost men who claimed there was no real farming left in the county. In the whole country for that matter. Something dishonest in all of it—parity, subsidies, not-so-discreet poisons that leaked into wells and aquifers, the backs of migrants.

Grace's seven-acre dream fell as always against her real wish list, which from the start had included wheat, corn, hay, straw, windrows, silos, tractors, balers, wagons, and all the young hands to make them go. And most of all a landscape that would roll away beyond her field of vision.

"It's cold," Jerry said. "Roll up the window."

"We don't have to roll. We just press."

"Roll, press, do it." Testy already and not even married.

Still, she couldn't make herself tell him that next week was going to be much too soon, that he'd been thrown among all the men roving in her future.

9. THE INCUBATOR BALLROOM

The barn was thick with people under the heat lamps radiating red from the steel hovers. The incubator, its doors open, sat like a huge and inefficient space heater in the middle, its empty egg trays turning slowly.

"Not married." The news spread quickly over the floor. The smooth cement had been dusted with dance wax bought by Aunt Michael, who feared the surface was not slippery enough, even for a Virginia reel.

"Not a barn dance," Ailene comforted her. "Just a dance in a barn." There was a makeshift table of saw horses and a sheet of plywood, which sagged under several dozen cylinders of salami and bologna and long bars of American cheese. And a tiered cake, another gift of her catering friends. The champagne was going to be pour-your-own-into-dixie-cups. After that, kegs of beer.

"Trust those two." Aunt Michael meant Grace and Eddie, who were agreeing it was too late for a parking plan. Cars were already scattered up and down both sides of the driveway and out along the river road. And more people coming. Eddie had sent Wendell down to the entrance to put out railroad flares.

"Why does he advertise her shame?" Grace could hear Aunt Michael working away on Ailene. "A pity and, yes, a disgrace."

"Think of this as the ballroom in Roanoke," Ailene told her. "Don't worry. They'll be married next week." Her evidence, the presents already opened, including extra toasters and salad bowls, and one place setting of silver inscribed G&J R. The setting was from Georgia, still complaining she'd been suckered by Aunt Michael, who had chosen the pattern and then showed up with a porcelain doll from a secondhand shop.

"It's all right," Grace comforted her while the big, black amplifiers began to work their vibrations into the oak timbers. "I'm only going to need one setting."

There had been a small group of the new Mason Hills people who stood well dressed and uncomfortable by the barn door waiting for a reception line to form. They had come out of curiosity and drifted away after awkward greetings. Grace could recall the names of only a few couples, and these seemed best defined by the interests of the wives. The husbands, who sold their talents closer to the city, held jobs too vague to lodge in memory.

There were the Clarkes, recently from Fairfax. She was doing her kitchen in French country, and more memorable for arriving and departing with a large box wrapped in silver paper and white ribbon. Mr. and Mrs. Vincent Villon also left quickly, though not before Mrs. Villon had explained the thrill of a new real-estate license. "I'd love to offer this place." Soon after that, the hearty Robinsons were on their way. The wife designed perennial borders. "We don't agree with what you're doing here," Mr. Robinson told Grace, "but, by God, we defend your right to do it."

Instead of playing alternate sets, the two bands had agreed to mix their sounds in a harmony of double volume. Ailene, fearing aural damage, had bits of Kleenex wadded in her ears. The Rices, upset by the aborted ceremony, had left before the musical riot, and Jerry, set adrift in the crowd by Grace, had turned to the champagne.

Star, worried that all the older people would be driven from the barn, went to the microphone to organize the Virginia reel that Aunt Michael had so feared. A caller was found and enough space cleared for two lines of eight dancers, but after a long interval of instruction, the thing still would not go. The reason was Annalee, who refused to accept the reel's permutations. Halfway through the dance she was still opposite Billy Johnson, though she'd started with him as her partner.

Now Grace was across from Michael, Star stood facing Eddie, and Ailene was lost in another mix-up. As the two lines came together to raise hands, Grace heard Star shout to her father: "See how the chromosomes are paired off now?" The caller gave up, and the fast, loose-hipped dancing of the agile young took over the floor again.

Grace saw her mother and father going off together. The sound of their arguing had never been so agreeable. Voices driven to exasperation only meant they were working again on the difficult accommodation their marriage had always been.

The volume knobs were spun up to ten and the party became palpable over all the houses of Mason Hills, and even across the river in Maryland. And rabbit and fox went to ground as headlights played up and down the driveway and into the vine-choked undergrowth.

Jerry came toward her, champagne sloshing, and backed her up against the incubator. His eyes were dark with censure as he watched the effeminate and suggestive undulations of the dancers, the floor packed with people eager to do the right and modern thing for the throbbing music. "I wouldn't even do that in a bedroom," he said.

She wouldn't answer, and his eyes bore in. "How about this?" he said. "When we're finished tonight, I'll put you inside this thing, shut the doors and leave you for nine months. If it works, we'll breed you right back again."

Grace slid down against the incubator, ducked under his arm, and danced across the floor, moving the way he disapproved of. Without a partner she imitated the thing Annalee was doing with Billy, hips pumping in a slow circle, as her hands moved up and down her body. Like soaping up in a shower. "You're doing the Wash," Annalee called to her.

Jerry caught her from behind, pulled her slinky arms to her sides and held her still. "After tonight," he said into her ear, "you'll be doing my wash."

No, she began to explain, it wasn't going to work out that way. "Maybe sometime."

"I don't know why I ever messed with you people," he said. And he was gone. Later, Grace learned he'd gotten into an argument with Tommer, who had been cruising back and forth on the river road in front of her driveway, patrolling the debauch for the Lord.

The crowd in the barn was working itself toward a sweaty frenzy. Hard to recognize the sound as music now but for the throbbing bass line, more like physical blows than differentiated notes. Her family had already left the party.

Grace walked out into the night, looked over honeysuckle, wild grapevine, and the prickly spines of locust saplings, down to the few remaining trees of the old woods. The electric thump and whine behind her was driving her toward the house. She caught a glimpse of Georgia walking past her upstairs window in one of her teddies, her arms stretched forward. Reaching out, Grace supposed, for invisible Wendell.

The place had been set back in time, its furniture and family sent back for another try. The reunion had done something for all of them, Grace thought, nipped the complacency of their sudden wealth. The new players like Wendell and Star didn't count for much. They seemed so easily replaceable. She could imagine the house again as a network of exciting bedrooms, even the master bedroom with her mother and father's easing argument taking them in that direction.

"Eddie, before our lights go out, I want everyone out of the barn."

"A party ends when it's ready. I'm not telling anyone to leave."

They'd been married to this kind of quibble for years. As Grace stood on the porch listening, it was clear to her they'd be using the same bed again. She imagined them as nature's willy-nilly lovers, commingled in a slow coitus, a gentler continuation of crossed purposes, each of them fighting off pleasure while pushing the other toward a release.

The noise from the barn was a nuisance now. Her father left Ailene and Aunt Michael in the kitchen and went down the hall. Grace followed outside, along the porch, and heard him speak as he entered his study.

"What are you doing here, Michael?"

She could see her cousin through the window, but could not hear his voice. Eddie sounded angry. "Well, you won't find it here." Again, Michael's answer was too low. "No!" her father said. "Out there! That's what matters! All those people in one place!" He was pointing toward the barn. "This is the time young people wait for. When the thing can go out of control. Then it's over. Do you understand?" He threw his arms up impatiently.

Grace heard a glass break at the other end of the house. She went back again along the porch, and heard her mother and aunt arguing in the kitchen. "Don't make me laugh. You shipped Michael up here whenever it was convenient. And we enjoyed him."

"Enjoyed? Is that what you call it?"

"Would he have been better off with you? The way you were carrying on?"

This part of Aunt Michael, alluded to, never fully explained, still intrigued Grace. Her parents' censure and her aunt's denial. Season after season, as Eddie had confessed of his sister, even after she was married, coaxing young men up to the hotel's bedrooms, while painting her life as a chaste idyll. As if the elegance of the ballroom cleansed the elevator ride.

"Don't turn this around," she said bitterly. "We're talking about your girls. Annalee out there going goggle-eyed at that gigolo farm boy. And Grace!" Aunt Michael gave the back of her hand to the ugliness of it all. "Have you noticed how short the boy's fingers are?"

The short fingers closed on Grace's arm. She spun around. "Not too short for your equipment," he said. "There's more we have to get straight." Jerry's upper lip was swollen and when he opened his mouth she saw each tooth outlined in liquid red. He pulled her by the arm off the porch and through the wild bower, and she agreed to sit in his truck and explain it all to him again.

Grace tried but it was coming out of an advice column. Ten ways to say good-bye. They worked for me. Not-so-artful excuses that cast all blame on her unworthy self, and made him a wounded hero, well rid of her. "No," she said. "Forget all that. I'll tell you why it isn't going to happen. It's because the way we're looking at each other right now is the same way we'd be looking if we were telling each other the truth. We don't even know when we're lying. We don't do anything real. Remember?"

She thought she might have broken through accidentally to some useful kernel. Not Jerry. He fired up the engine and then sprayed cinders at cars along the driveway. "No," she said. "I'm staying here." He slid onto the river road, fishtailed close to an oncoming car, and as he braked to avoid the ditch, Grace threw herself against the door handle and tumbled out of the truck. She was up and running across the floodplain toward her home.

The pickup's headlights turned into the field. Grace looked back and saw that a man was coming after her at an easy lope, more menacing than a sprint, a feral calculation of their relative speed and endurance. And something danger-ous in his hand. Coming out of the trees and into the tangled undergrowth of her own property, she struggled ahead and made a hiding place under honeysuckle.

The man became a wandering voice. Muffled and distant it didn't quite sound like Jerry or Tommer. Whoever it was would have had to step on her to find her. She was that well hidden under the vegetable blanket that covered all of her land. The beacon of noise from the barn had stopped.

"I'm waiting for you, Grace."

Not waiting, she thought. Hunting. He seemed to have gone on beyond her and then circled back again. "Are you scared of me?" This was a voice from another direction. There were two of them.

Maybe a half hour later, her heart at peace again, it seemed unbelievable that her imagination had turned the morning's gentle groom into a masher waving a wrench overhead. She stood and spoke into the darkness, "Is anyone there?"

Nothing. She began to move again. In the homemade jungle her progress was a slow hand-over-hand grappling with the tangled growth and brambles. Impenetrable thickets of wild rose forced her to one side and another. She was sure she had climbed and descended several inclines until she came to the taller trees again, and realized the steep places had all been parts of the same hill.

She'd gone nowhere. Her farm was a challenge, a seven-acre maze. She turned back into it again and was quickly hidden once more in the thick cover. Enveloped in the vines and scrub, she could move all night and never reach the house. She could be lost on her own meagre plot.

For the moment she believed she was heading toward the house. "I'm coming," she announced to her distant family. There was cursing behind and in front of her. As she crawled away from their argument, she heard Jerry and Tommer call each other disgusting names. They'd try to crush each other's skulls with their bare fists, she supposed. And later in the week they'd sit down to swiss steaks in the lunch room and share vulgar little details of the game-farm girl one of them had solved. Tommer, always the irritated plowman, as her father had said, with religion or without.

Her acres stretched out before her now, blocking her way to the house. As blind to her progress as if she'd been standing in seven-foot corn. In adjacent fields to either side of her she might be passing crops of wheat, alfalfa, soy beans. Grace covered her face against the stalks that beat against her arms and legs.

Over how many more hills, beyond how many harvests, was the house asleep and waiting? Each bedroom, even the attic, holding someone who would spring awake to hear her story. She could knock on any door for a willing audience.

Michael had anticipated being woken that night. As soon as he'd heard the wedding was postponed he supposed she'd come to him with all her homely secrets. Not to ask advice, just to share the latest with him as she'd done before—news of the day or plan of the year. And quite like her to come at a compromising hour, long after Star had gone to sleep in Annalee's room. He was prepared to scold her a little, and send her back upstairs to her own bed.

Grace had always been clever at putting the house to her use. She'd know how to make all the covering sounds that would take her family off alert, relax them into their pillows. A little water running in the bathroom sink, the click of her bedroom door latch, the squeak of the tight top drawer of her bureau. All the innocent noises of retiring for the night.

Then down the steps and through the passageway to his room, her footfall hidden under the little cacophony of clocks striking the hour. His Aunt Ailene had brought back the two table models and the grandfather, once more in the front hall, parlor, and stairway landing. Their three sets of chimes uncannily striking in the same old sequence as if they'd never forgotten which was expected to be prompt and which tardy, their old duty on the game farm.

When her knock came, the clocks had just finished with three A.M. He could make out her slender figure in the dark room as she came in and closed the door behind her. "It's Grace," she said. The news was she'd had a transforming day, had gone from the aborted wedding on a trip to a great farm where she'd lost her sense of direction, wandered through golden wheat and endless soy beans, and wound up in her old room off the kitchen.

He wasn't going to let her confuse him with riddles. As his eyes adjusted he saw that her nightgown was an undershirt, and no modesty of protecting hands over the dark triangle beneath it. Her arms were folded casually across her front. She did not seem to be flaunting her half-naked body so much as presenting it as a matter of family fact, something that had been returned to the house along with all the furniture.

Why should he be made the lecturing prude? Staring across the room, wishing he could dress her with his eyes, he demanded, "What would someone think, coming in here now? You better hope they're all asleep."

"Don't be a stiff, Michael. I only came to be sociable." The patent falsehood of that made him laugh. He sat up to full attention, sheets and comforter pulled up around him because he slept in no more than she did. Provoking him, presenting herself as an alternative to Star, and damn the physical comparison. She had nerve. A straight sapling offered up in place of the fancy pneumatic raft on which he'd been drifting for several years.

But going on in such a matter-of-fact, sexless way. "What's funny?" she asked him, reaching along the wall, not taking her eyes off him.

"No, don't turn the light on." The longer she stood there the higher the contrast between her skin and shadows. He must not soften his voice. Give her the least license and she might come striding across the floor on those long, pale stilts, and expect to be taken down beside him.

"What were you and my father arguing about?" she asked.

"He found me poking around in his library."

"That wouldn't bother him."

"He said the party was about to do its worst, and I was missing it. Why talk about your father at this hour?"

Her mouth became a black circle before settling back into a firm, dark line. She'd begun to say, "He likes it that you and I . . ." but must have thought better of finishing. Michael squirmed on the mattress, trying to reverse the effect she was having. "What are you doing, Michael?"

He looked down at the covers, ashamed of what was happening to him. It was Grace's ordinariness. That was the problem, the thing that excited him. So casual in presentation of her unexceptional self. As if his bedroom, even with her in it, were a dull chamber in need of simple conversation. It didn't seem to matter to her what his reaction was, and this, too, was a provocation.

"Do you like what we're doing, Michael?"

"We haven't done anything," he said sharply.

"It came up so fast, as if we'd fertilized it."

Too late, he understood she meant the vegetation closing around the house. He's the one in the family who knows her body is as wild as her farm, that she cultivates the wildness. In a single day she had freed herself, and reinvented her life for a fertile but cropless future. Her defiance was part of the attraction; she'd defy any of them and nurture what was sown by the wind.

Star was miles away, upstairs. She can't help it that her

beauty is the greedy kind that demands attentions, competitions, victories. And Grace can't help it that hers demands nothing, and is for that reason impossible to ignore. He glanced down to where his covers had swollen and quickly looked up again.

What was the matter, she wanted to know, did her being there upset him?

"No," he said, "why should you bother me?"

She told him she couldn't think of a reason, shifting her weight from one leg to the other.

He flinched and fired a question to hold her in place. "Jerry? What did he say?"

"Blamed all of us. Gave me the 'you people' treatment. 'Should have known better than to mess with you people.' And, 'what could you expect from people who'd hunt ducks in the summertime?' This way he's not losing much. Just the wacko bitch of the game farm." Her mouth became a black circle again, and he supposed she'd amused herself.

She came a few steps into the room and stopped. "He probably thought he could put a stop to all this."

"Are you going to stay in one place?" he asked quickly.

"Yes," she told him, "I like it here." But she was coming forward again, explaining she was going to stay no matter what her father decided. "When you don't do anything, everybody gets interested." It wouldn't be lawyers and land sharks anymore, but botanists, zoologists, the whole ecological caboodle. They'd all want a piece of her project now that the law couldn't stop her.

The Mason preserve. With bets on a hundred little wars in progress. Honeysuckle or poison ivy to choke ailanthus before ailanthus took the sun from maples? Or shallow, thirsty maples to parch the evergreens? And what mammals to prevail? Grace, fox, squirrel, opossum, vole. A decade would be soon enough for another inventory. He listened in disbelief. She meant to bury herself in her small wilderness.

She'd done nothing, and the battles had been joined. Another year or two and the house itself, already covered in green, would look, from a distance, like a swelling in a mole's tunnel. So Grace might burrow away while the local boys came to hunt her, hoping to put an end to her singularity.

"Are you trying to hide here?"

"Trying? There's no effort. Nature's growing up around me."

Grace came across the room to the bed, thicket of pubes at his eye level and moving forward, right into his outstretched hand. She fell down beside him and was immediately busy at gently urgent work. Taking liberty from one end of him to the other. Inviting him here and there. A sexual instructor, he thought, not so much out to conquer as to demonstrate the possibilities. She was taking him right through love's dictionary, lingering at startling entries, and her old caveat was more moaned than spoken: "This should only happen once." Some time before dawn she vanished.

At breakfast Aunt Ailene pressed grapefruit juice on him. "The others had theirs, Michael. Take your medicine. The bride hasn't come down yet." When Grace did arrive in the kitchen, she told her worried family it was just as well the wedding hadn't happened. In fact, it wasn't going to happen. She walked behind Michael's chair, put a hand on his shoulder and said, "If he wasn't already taken, this would be the one for me." Putting them off the trail, he understood, by going directly to it. "Did you sleep as well as I did, Michael?"

Each of the fancy things Grace had done the night before were digested again with the tart juice. He looked at her scratched hands and arms and unblinking eyes that admitted nothing. No damage done.

Michael disagreed. He'd allowed himself to be pleased in ways that amazed and now obliged him. Her chin was thrust forward in belligerent command of the day. This and the way her lips pressed together in a satisfied line only added to his disgrace. Once more, on a morning after, he found his cousin unappealing, not someone to be loved but maneuvered into a private room, whispered to, thanked. She was rawboned and chapped, a pitiable sight next to her sisters and Star.

Through the day the family came and went, using the kitchen as the common room where travel plans were made, changed, and made again. Since Grace was not going to marry, they were all poised to scatter. Ailene and Eddie had made no announcement, though it was clear they'd be travelling together. Back and forth between Mason Hills and Roanoke until they decided which home would be sanitarium to their healing marriage.

Michael's mother was feinting at early departure. Georgia and Annalee couldn't have been kinder, fussing over Grace's disappointment. Georgia suggested filling the empty hours ahead with good works for other people. "To get your mind off yourself." Annalee promised not to leave before Grace was well.

Grace winked at him. Not a lover's signal. More a conspiracy of boredom with all the naïve concern floating in the house.

"She must be crushed."

"She doesn't let it show. Think what's going on inside."

All her loving, tiresome family with the exception of her father. He must have known that her heart was alive again because he was giving her chores as he'd done when she was a child too puffed up with her importance on the farm. "Grace, clean up the barn. It's your mess."

Ailene jumped to protect her. "Can't you see? She's numb. Leave her alone."

"No. It's fine," Grace said. "Michael can help me."

"Michael's got to pack," his mother said.

Star looked puzzled. "Are we leaving? We wouldn't abandon Grace, would we?"

"You're not staying here." His mother was fixing his collar. "Did you dress in a stupor?" She gave Star a foul look, as if she might have drugged her son with the forbidden debauch while the rest of the house slept. Michael pushed away her interfering fingers.

"They can stay as long as they like," Grace said. She was on her way to the barn. "Come on, Michael."

"Come on, come on," his mother mocked. Did you know that's what the Portuguese call us? 'Comeonesh.' People who say come all the time." Instead of calling attention to Grace, his mother only reminded herself of the sad affair with her Portuguese caller, and Ailene helped her into the next room for a sob and a Kleenex.

Grace's command had failed; she had to drag Michael away rudely. Scarcely out of earshot of the others she asked, "Did I leave you in a stupor?" leaning affectionately against him on their way through the wild bower. Before they entered the barn she had already given him his release: "There's nothing for you to be ashamed of. There's a preserve here and I'm part of it. Nothing is going to be clipped, nothing is going to be killed." She was a lonely person, he thought, who had begun to behave like an animal where light is closed out and there is no longer a need for rules.

Grace walked methodically up and down the floor, pushing beer cans and paper cups ahead of her. He watched in fascination as she transformed herself into the hired hand again, behind a wide broom, someone he could be comfortable with as they worked together on a project to satisfy someone else—her father. It was always in this cast that she seemed most desirable. She could have been a woman at the

next position in a factory, her mechanical activity, the pumping of an arm, or foot on a treadle, denying any inkling of
sexual strategy while perspiration gathered and flowed down
the shallow valley at the front of her T-shirt, and she cut him
forever from her life with a careless word and the back of her
hand.

He studied the simplicity of Grace, her endearing belief
that the value of a life could be calculated as the sum of its
farm chores. He watched her mouth go slack as she concen-
trated on this one, the mere sweeping of a floor, reducing his
want of a clear conscience to something less important than
the rattle of aluminum and the squashing of paper cups.

After the floor was clean, she asked him to help take
down the hovers hanging from the beams. They worked
quietly for some time before Grace began to drop rapid questions on him from a high rung of her ladder. "Do you know
what my family thinks about you? Do you know what they're
saying about Star? Do you know where she's leading you? Do
you have any idea where you're going?" Questions only she
could detonate.

"A sweet boy, that's what they think. Who's grown into a
waster. That you made a myth for yourself, and now you're
living down to it.... And Star's one of those Charlottesville
gypsies trading her big ideas for food, clothing, and shelter.... They all think she's taking you to the end of your
story."

"Where's that?"

"Nowhere, if I understand what you've been telling us."

"And what do you think?"

"That I won't have to come looking tonight."

He bumped the ladder hard with his hand as if he hoped
Grace might fall. Fussing with a knot, she didn't bother to
look down as he strode away.

He welcomed the coming of night, his opportunity to prove his cousin vain and mistaken. Neither would he ask Star down to his room. Likely as not she'd refuse anyway, not caring to upset the Mason calm. She'd told him, "When your mother's gone there'll be a new atmosphere," as if she'd deprived the house of love's oxygen. Star even blamed the failed wedding on air poisoned by his mother.

Now the household was all down on Star, and he'd done little to defend her. They'd accepted Ailene's judgment that the girl's knowledge was wide but shallow and thus could only be used to impress, never to enlighten. What he and Star were going to prove to the world had not quite been defined, though he still believed there was a bright career ahead of them in which intellectual enthusiasm turned into something practical, that is, into money.

For the moment, Grace's new wilderness surrounded and held the family. He and Star included. And what they were all doing was being done to please Grace. While they appeared to be giving her advice and warning, they had actually been taking her direction, made witness to the farm's remains, reproaching themselves in their new fortunes, and staying on for her signal that all had worked out for the best.

Instead of an encouraging sign, there was her erratic wandering over the land. After her little lecture from the top of the ladder, she had pretended to throw him into the generality of her family. "None of you see what's happening." Claiming that she'd brought the house and small acreage past the point of danger into an easement in which neither family nor outsiders could destroy it. "It wasn't just a legal fight, Michael. That's where you're as blind as the others."

"She thinks she's won a battle for our souls," he told her

———

father, holding Grace's vanity up for puncture, and probing for his uncle's suspicion.

Eddie riffling the pages of the book he held, gathering knowledge with his laser eye, swivelled in his chair completely away from Michael's nervous gaze, and began to talk about mallards: "You could tell their sex by their voices. That didn't work with Grace, did it Michael?"

"Sir?"

"On the phone, people were always calling her Mr. Mason." He thumbed across the pages again, placed the book down, and still facing his desk, leaned back to stare at the ceiling. So that a nose appeared to Michael to grow out of a forehead, and words rose slowly from an invisible mouth in a pointed argument whose base was speculation. Composing a homemade corruption like one of his Roman poets.

"You,
you, Michael
you're the old familiar,
the one Grace thought so much of.
Remember, saving you from bats and snakes?
Until she got old enough to hide you in her room.
So what kind of surprise have you got with you this time?
Not just a pretty scholar to tease us all with a lot of paradox."

"We were invited to a wedding."

"Wedding? That wasn't a wedding. It was a ruse, a trick Grace played on herself. No, she wants something easier, don't you think? Something that won't require ceremony."

"We were invited to a wedding," Michael repeated. His

uncle was having none of it, continuing in his own line. "She wasn't much on travel, was she? Pennsylvania once for a farm exhibition. The others went off the usual way, looking for excitement in strangers. Grace's pleasure was always to hide in the familiar, wouldn't you say?"

He wouldn't say. And his uncle wouldn't bother to turn. Michael went looking for Star to tell her they'd be leaving in the morning. He wanted to get on with the night in his own room, have it over, and sun shining on a victory breakfast, a silent toast in sour juice to a night of easy abstinence.

Lying back on his narrow bed he felt unfairly accused, like the rogue in the last movie he'd seen with Star, a protagonist with flesh for a moral compass, and faulted by his heroine: "For God's sake, Harry, every time the thing points north you follow it."

Within the hour he changed his mind. He ought to go and tell her just what he thought, prove to her face that her test was easily passed. Shock her into a new respect, straighten the warp in her thinking. It would take tiptoeing and whispering to carry it off, and a long wait until the only other sounds in the house were the quarter-hour chimes.

The stairs would be no difficulty. But there was the creaky upper hallway and the chance of open doors. Waiting on his bed, the prospect of stealth began to undermine his purpose. His mood kept retreating. From the resolve of anger to petulance, to annoyance, and at last, a calm dissatisfaction and simple wish to be understood by Grace as a decent man and her friend.

On the stairway's first landing he was frozen in place by someone's midnight trip to the bathroom, and a drumming in his chest. Safer to turn and go back. No, he was climbing again, and slipping along the hall a bit recklessly. Not led by the disreputable compass; he was certain of that. But by the subtler and more demanding direction of his heart. He wanted to confess and be confessed to. Not to spoil the sanctuary they shared. To reassure himself that it would always be here, and that it depended on no more than an honest word between them. And the word was not flesh.

She had been waiting for him, standing in the dim light of her window. "I was getting a little chilly," she apologized, tweaking the shoulders of her flannel night shift as if its high-bibbed neck and ankle length carried modesty to a false and inconvenient extreme. He ought to say something right away so that she wouldn't embarrass herself. Silly ever to have thought he'd want to shame her.

"I'm not staying," he warned.

"No, you're not," she surprised him, turning his decision into a ruling of her own.

"Listen!" she said.

Michael could hear nothing.

"They're talking again. Come here."

She put her ear to the wall of her mother's room. He moved beside her and pressed his cheek next to hers against the cool plaster. Her pupils were swollen like a cat's.

They could hear Uncle Eddie say, "He won't be here much longer. I'm certain of it."

"I wish he'd get that girl out of here." Ailene's voice was equally clear.

"The headboard's right there," Grace whispered, pointing down at the wall. "They must be on the bed."

Ailene was asking how Eddie could be so positive.

"The girl is history," he said. "Have you been dieting again? Don't read diet books. Not healthy."

"She'll be here in the morning, won't she. That's not history. No, put your hand here. I've tried to like her, but I just can't."

Eddie said something about university gypsies, Star, a throwback, a brief time when glamour had been traded for a patina of knowledge.

"Disloyalty," was Ailene's complaint. "She'd sooner impress you than Michael. Please, Eddie, you never got that right. That's not lovely, it just hurts. Put your hand here."

"This is none of my business." Michael raised his head.

"It is," Grace corrected, pulling him back.

"I'm telling you!" Eddie was clearly annoyed. "They won't be here much longer."

"I'm worried for Michael."

His aunt's sigh sounded like resignation. But resignation to what? His problematic life? His uncle's clumsy hand? "Of course, for Grace too." Michael had taken his ear from the wall, but Ailene's voice, raised a pitch, still penetrated the lathe and plaster. "We overreacted, Eddie. They were only children then. We made them so wary of each other."

"Let's think about something else." The voices trailed off to a murmuring.

"Do they get the last word?" Grace wondered aloud. All Michael could think to do was shake her hand. Absurd. Their hands passed, slipped along one another's wrists, and up each other's arms. Then her head was pressed in his palms. Her hair flared out between his fingers.

"What are you doing?"

He wasn't sure. He supposed, he said, it was a way to hold all of her. "Your ideas, everything." Her refuge, her separateness, all the words in her brain. Her face lit the way to all her extremities.

He held on this way, backing her across the room. A shared responsibility; if he was guiding, she was pulling. Moments later, naked and huddled together as if with the blessings of the establishment, they made another pact. Absolutely the last time this would be allowed between them. He felt safe and honorable, having interrupted the urgency to consider its meaning. In a family, extremes of distance and intimacy are both despised. The best would be led to the edge of broken covenants.

"Michael. I know you're in there. Michael, answer me." A light came on in the hall. Star was at the door.

"What's the matter?" Annalee had been roused.

No time to prepare a scene of innocent conversation. They were hardly able to pull the covers around them before Star came into the room.

Annalee screamed. Star was somewhat calmer. "Bitch!" she said. "Inbreeding bitch! Come on, Michael. You didn't want this." As if he'd been unfairly seduced and was already eligible for pardon.

The house came awake. Other feet were padding along the hall, and his mother was on her way down from the garret. Eddie and Ailene appeared in the doorway. Wendell yelled from Georgia's room, "Is someone sick?" and Star called back, "Yes! Yes!"

His mother arrived and, unable to dissolve the scene by staring at it, called her son pathetic, and Grace, upcountry trash. The others, agape, must have been waiting for contrition and correction. But naked, how could Michael move until they all went away?

"This is my room," Grace remembered.

They went out and shut the door to argue in the hall about what had happened. Ailene drew blame down on everyone. "How could we have been so blind?"

His mother had a narrower target: the loosely raised niece, the one who had never set foot in the hotel. Anyway, what did they expect in a house where everyone was given a million dollars whether they deserved it or not? She must have liked the sound of that. As he dressed he could hear her asking them all the same thing, one after another, until Eddie asked her please to shut up.

Grace overwhelmed the censors. She took control in the morning, routing any group of two or three who gathered in the common rooms to chat in low voices about the problem here. "There is no problem here. Come on mum, let's get you packing. All of you have lives of your own, don't you?"

Ailene had sent Annalee around to strip the beds. Grace countermanded. "I'll take care of the wash after you've gone." In the laundry room the big tub of the ancient washing machine had already been filled with the hottest water, and Clorox poured with a heavy hand. The agitator paddled purifying fumes into the front hall and up the stairway.

"Turn that thing off!" Grace ordered. Annalee obeyed.

Grace's domain. Her father and mother would only be visitors after today. Watching Michael's mouth go sour as he put the breakfast juice to his lips, Grace took the glass from him and poured it into the sink. Then left him alone to make peace with his Starblanket.

As she went through the halls remarking the things her mother had returned, she could hear Star saying: "So you've come full circle. So what? Where else could you begin but at the beginning?" No tirade of betrayal, only a little more of her easing sophistry. Grace believed her father wrong about Michael's other. Not history at all, but a lovely calculator who, for the time being, could draw Michael back to her with appealing solutions.

Grace kept circulating through the house, discouraging

collusive whispering, forcing them toward departure. They could worry about her from a distance. The land was hers to manage now, what was left of it. She could not produce on a large scale; she would conserve on a small one.

Flush in their separate millions, they had ceded her the last acres. The conservation easement had already been drafted, making a permanent home for crayfish in the muddy creek bed, and a cover, in perpetuity, for one or two deer chased across the open lawns of Mason Hills by terriers. A botanical riot and home to whatever animal, native or immigrant, should stay and survive.

"Grace's biosphere," her father called it. The contents of the house were something else. These were to be shared by all. She went on through the rooms, letting her fingers play on the scrollwork and finials of an eighteenth-century highboy, on the panelling of an armoire of alleged importance, on the soft curve of a sleigh bed of no special worth except that she liked it, on the varnished Moran.

That night, with all of them packed off to the south, she began her first night alone as curator of the Mason museum. Overseer, too, of the thing left behind in their minds, the phantom painting of her and Michael, arms entwined, and drawn from life. Now part of the permanent collection. Not to be framed or hung.

She could count on it now; they would always come back as her father had predicted, to reunite and recollect the game farm. And to monitor any deviant behavior in her closing wilderness. Grace had no fear of the loneliness they predicted for her. A mad woman of Mason Hills, graying and wrinkling in senseless isolation.

Through the new growth of wisteria over her bedroom

window, Grace watched cars moving easily back and forth along the river road, throwing shadows into the woods. Michael has been freed. When he breaks away from Charlottesville from time to time, he'll find comfort here.

Jerry was out there, beyond the new estates, waiting to be sure the extra vehicles were gone from her driveway. And other young men would be circling. Beyond them, more coming. No hurry. She knew that sanctuary was a vacuum, and nature would demand an end to her peculiarity.

KARAGHALA'S DAUGHTER

"Kara for Karaghala. Nagy for Pronagy. How do you like it?"
Johanna's father thrust out his chin to see if the name would
suit his face. Observing the fit of a new white linen jacket on
his long-waisted figure, she couldn't help thinking he should
have been in pictures.

"Hollywood?" she asked.

"Virginia," he said. "When you graduate."

"And who will I be in Virginia?"

"You'll be Jo Nagy. You'll live with me beside a mill-
stream, and drive a Karmann-Ghia." He chuckled until his
mouth and eyes became the resolute slits of his will.

And six months later her father's prediction had come
true in every detail. There were twenty acres, bought sight
unseen, on a creek that ran into the Potomac. The Karmann-
Ghia was red.

"It might be like the folktale," she warned. She meant the
one in which a widower takes his daughter from the city to
live and work in a mill. One by one, the teeth of its wooden
gears crack. All its wheels are worn smooth. Nothing turns,
and their idyll is ground into country poverty.

"We have more than we'll ever need," her father promised her.

Karaghala's life had progressed as an odyssey indifferent to law. As a boy in Budapest he had lived on the Buda side, the hilly half of the double city, where he and friends rode down in the mornings on sleds to their academies along the Danube. But he had dreamed of racing down the same slopes on ice skates.

One winter he had beaten down a narrow double track in the snow. It rained, and the water froze on his piste, and he fairly flew down the trail, leaping into a snowbank at the bottom to stop himself. For days he amazed them with his daredevil trip. But one morning another boy skied back and forth across his lanes, ruining them for skates. Karaghala fought him with snow, then ice balls, then fists. He knocked the culprit down, and the boy's head made a bad and final sound.

Sixteen, Karaghala was not charged with murder. He was sent off to Austria and then Switzerland. The Hungarian government changed, and shortly afterward his family had trouble with the new regime. There was no return for him. A relief agency found him a home in America.

Johanna's father wouldn't travel in the same vehicle with her anymore. Her mother and brother had been killed two years before in an auto on the Pulaski Skyway. Johanna had been away at college. It was hard for Karaghala to think of the deaths as accidental. His wife and son had been in his own limousine, behind darkened glass.

He drove south in a car just like it, Johanna in her Karmann-Ghia. He carried the hand luggage—the guns with the harsh German names and a case of his city-strength roach killer. She brought the dog, Georgette.

In New Jersey the guns had never been loaded, though Karaghala had kept ammunition, the cruellest kind of lead, which, he explained, could hit a finger and explode a hand. He sounded as if he knew from experience. Johanna was certain he didn't.

"We won't need the guns," she said.

"Yes," he agreed. "Because we'll have them."

"And they don't have roaches in the country."

"I'm just retiring," he told her, "not giving up."

The Virginia retreat, an old frame farmhouse, turned out to have almost no driveway. "Twenty acres to hide in," Karaghala said, "and here I am a target right on the road."

Waiting for the moving van, Johanna and her father walked their fence line. "Too many holes," he said. "What's that?"

"A chicken coop," she told him.

"Where are the hens?"

"Horses jump over it."

"Onto my land?"

They walked on, Karaghala finding rotten posts, rusty and broken wire, the whole fence just a trellis for honeysuckle, and more chicken coops. "Invitations," he said. "I haven't invited anyone."

Johanna held his hand and smoothed his collar. She was going to have to explain him to the neighbors. The guns were closet pieces. He scarcely knew how to load them. He not only braked for animals but spoke to them; he used bubble bath. But how could a daughter say all this about her father without betraying him?

There was no Doberman, no German shepherd. They had Georgette, a mongrel with short black-and-brown hair, a stray that Karaghala had rescued in Bayonne, a dog with no country manners. On her first day at large in Virginia Georgette had come home after dark and dropped a chicken part at their feet. They had to tie her in the yard.

The movers, when they arrived, were rude. Their procession over the threshold continued long after the house was comfortably full of furniture, and they sneered at Karaghala's fussing over each bump and scratch. He was counting on Johanna to see that claims were filed for loss and breakage.

She wouldn't be the one to tell him it was mostly worthless stuff, cheap wood joined with staple guns. In front of the movers she felt her father was again a refugee, though this time he came with money. Plenty of it, he liked to say. Unaware of his past, how could they be charmed?

He'd told her often how he sailed from Le Havre as a boy. The relief people had pinned the address of his new family to his clothes in three places, as if they'd been mailing a package. On board he ripped the tags off, arriving in America with an independence that frightened his new parents in New Jersey.

Johanna imagined a couple too old for her father's cunning. For two years he'd suffered their awkward pity, their advice about study habits and how to behave with girls. With sufficient grammar for citizenship he fled their home to become a hustler on the meanest streets of Bayonne.

There he moved among longshoremen, his arm covered with watches, wrist to elbow, under the red and black stripes of the last of the Hungarian shirts he'd brought with him. He took such pleasure in this memory she wished she had seen the shirt. It had been the sign of his arrival on the docks with the smallware he fenced, the watches that ticked or did not, the jewels that were or were not jewels. Because he had guaranteed things only to be what they were, his tough customers bought with a smile and at their risk, and he was never brained with a tire iron or dumped in the river.

"I couldn't get promoted in the shirt," he always said. At some point it had vanished—infested, or stolen in a Y, or thrown away when he began running dockside errands for men who drove up and down the northern end of the Jersey Turnpike in long cars. "Karaghala," he recalled them saying, "you make us laugh." As a prank he had once chained two of their bumpers together at a funeral.

"Do you love pecans?" Karaghala asked Johanna their first morning in Virginia. "You know, I've always loved pecans." He was surveying his new domain from the back door, as if just discovering a reason for owning country acres. The next day he sent Johanna to the county seat to declare his intention to plant a grove of pecan trees. The extension agent sent her home again, saying it wouldn't be approved; pecans had never been a cash crop there.

In their new home Johanna tried to walk in her mother's steps, timing Karaghala's eggs carefully and observing the old rules of laundry day. After ironing she rolled up each pair of his shorts inside a T-shirt so he could take them from his drawer together. "Hygiene twin-packs," Johanna called them. She was learning to lighten old rituals by renaming them. Her father could be very bad about changing his clothes.

When Karaghala saddened in the evenings, she played backgammon with him, but never allowed his losses to become heavy. She cheerfully swept the board clear, even in the middle of a game, before he grew upset with his luck. And she made the vodka toddy for his bedside table, the same sleeping potion her mother had prepared, with a teaspoon of sugar and a garlic clove.

For the first weeks Johanna did their marketing alone. When she finally coaxed her father into the village for chores, the postmistress said, "Hello, Mr. Nagy," before he introduced himself, and a grocer asked, "How's that pretty daughter?"

He came home right away to tell her, "They already know us here."

"Of course," she said. "We're the new people by the mill, who want to plant nut trees."

First to visit them was a young man from the hunt, Roger, who sold stocks for a living, and wanted to put Johanna on a horse. His black hair and perfect teeth reminded her of her brother. He was talking to her father but looking at her. "We gallop down your hill," he said. "We come in up there and jump out at the bottom. What kind of dog is that?"

"A Bayonne," Karaghala said.

Roger told them about the sort of people he hunted with. "A little reckless. Along the Irish lines, if you know what I mean."

"I've skated down steeper than that," Karaghala said.

Roger made plans with Johanna for a riding lesson at his stable. During the riding lesson he made plans with her for dinner at a riverside restaurant. The meal was expensive and candlelit, and after dessert he said, "Your barn or mine?" A miscalculation. She sat stonily until he asked about her father.

"Retired," she said. "But he wants to make a forest."

"The tree-farm scam! I know all about it," Roger said. "The seedlings are free. You get a farm-use rate on your land. Plant and put your feet up. So you all are into Christmas trees!"

He went on with analysis and advice: Stay away from blue spruce; too slow. Put your rows far enough apart to get a bush hog through. You'll lose some to the deer. Prune if you want full trees.

Wearying, she ordered brandy, and told Roger something about land use—about her father's landfill in New Jersey, a great cavity bulldozed from banks of barren red earth, where small towns and trash companies had paid to bring their garbage. Each year as they closed his hole in the landscape he depreciated its value until filled, levelled, and written down to zero; he sold it to developers as the greensward and recreational park of a huge new housing tract.

"He'll want to leave some trails through his pines," Roger said. "Nobody around here closes their land."

"He isn't doing Christmas trees," Johanna told him. "He wants pecans."

"If he plants pecans, he can play with the seedlings," Roger said. "His great-grandchildren may enjoy the nuts." And he whispered into her ear, "If he has great-grandchildren."

She'd already told this man too much about her father. It was a kind of betrayal even to accept another appointment with him. But he was the only one she knew here, the one who'd be taking their story to the neighbors. He was a man who could be kept in check, she thought, the kind whose hand could be removed from her chest or lifted from her knee and remain chastened for a whole evening.

Johanna had always feared that her popularity, or any small celebrity, could make Karaghala's life more visible. Shuffling, head down, through high school, she had told friends what she'd heard at home: "He's a magician with money. He pulls it out of the air."

In high school Johanna had dated no one. At university

she learned she could kiss a man deeply and still come home without shame. At home her father asked her blunt questions. When he began to offer guidelines for behavior, to list the things a woman could do to satisfy a man without fouling herself, she was appalled, not by the limits he set but by the things he could say in front of her. "Have a good time," he always told her, until his notion of a proper boyfriend turned into the real thing—arms, legs, and a mouth.

In Virginia it was going to be different. If she called herself Nagy she could do as she pleased. But a week later Roger phoned again and said, "Listen. I know who you are. Meet me at the mill."

His car was parked off the road. With his voice muffled by the sound of water moving through the old stone race, he said, "Your name is Pronagy. A friend of mine at the motor-vehicle office did your license transfers. Don't tell your father he's been found out."

Johanna laughed in Roger's face. Did he think he was dealing with the mob? She could explain, but he might not catch the humor and high spirit of it if she told how before his real-estate coup Karaghala had run a little travel agency in Newark. For city sportsmen. Hunting trips, that sort of thing. Occasionally there were bookings on phantom spur airlines into closed hotels.

Instead of that she told how in their family her father had always been a kind of folk hero, ruled by the magic of his own invention, though now he was simply a man mourning his wife and son, a man with time to stop and help a turtle across a road. She was letting her fingers play across the distance between them, remembering Karaghala's question when she'd returned from their first dinner: "You let this man touch you?"

Roger seemed to be asking for social data. "You must have been popular in college," he said. "What sorority?"

"No sorority," Johanna told him.

In her last year at university she had accepted election as class treasurer, though she knew she'd been chosen more for the line of her cheek and lip than for her ability to match dues with the cost of a prom. "Daddy used to ask where I kept the money," she said. "Just a joke. By then he was a very wealthy man. So now you know everything."

"They don't grow pecan trees in northern Virginia," Roger said.

"Now they do," she told him. "He can wait for his forest and call it a farm." She explained how the agricultural agent had relented when Karaghala read to him from his tree book: "Thomas Jefferson planted pecan seeds at Monticello, and gave some to George Washington. Pecans are among the oldest trees at Mount Vernon."

"Don't worry," Roger said. "I'll pretend your name is Nagy. I'll try not to call your house anymore. I won't tell anyone else." He said he was planning another ride for them, a trip across the valley and halfway up the mountain. They'd pack a lunch and look down on the hunt territory from a new altitude. "I want you to call me," he said, "when you're ready." His unencouraged hand slipped from her shoulder, down her arm, and into his own lap.

When Johanna did call Roger two weeks later, he was barely cordial, and was not at all sure there was an extra horse. "In your barn or mine?" she asked, and he said all right, there was probably a mount for her. But he couldn't come to pick her up. She'd have to meet him at the stable.

"This is Jo Nagy," he told his groom. "She'll want something quiet." He feared that her suède boots were going to smell of horse, that her fashion jeans would not be heavy enough to keep the stirrup leathers from pinching her legs, that her remarkably thin shirt would not keep her warm.

"I want to return you in good condition," he told her, and on their way up the mountain he confessed to having done some more research on her father. "What was it like growing up with him?"

"We weren't freaks," she told him. "We had normal lives."

"Daddy took you to the office?"

"Once or twice. That's average isn't it?" She remembered a glass door stencilled crudely "HUNTING UNLIMITED," a phone, a desk, and her mother's dismay that there were no posters, no travel brochures, only little white flyers, hunting regulations from dozens of counties, scattered around the room. Her father entertained Johanna with his phone work, shifting voices from one call to the next, facile as a comedian doing impersonations.

"He wanted to know if I let you touch me," she said.

Roger asked her please not to let her feet slip forward in the stirrups. It could be dangerous.

"He noticed you don't call anymore."

"If you force your heels down," Roger said, "you can't get in trouble."

They rode to a rock ledge where she spread a blanket for a recumbent meal, and Roger folded it again, saying it would serve best as a cushion.

It was a marvellous view he'd brought them to. Like a quilt, she said, in tans and greens, stitched with stone and board fencing. That was nice, he said, though it was hard for him not to think of all those patches in the valley as investment squares.

An amiable man, she decided, who had calculated the odds against him and now wouldn't play. She poured grape juice and said, "Pretend this is wine," and told a story about her father.

"In the city," she explained, "rich or poor, you live with cockroaches. City people know roaches the way country people know ticks. But ticks come to you. Roaches are escape artists; you have to be fast to catch them. When we were still very poor, living in the tenements, I used to grab them and put dots of paint on their backs and then let them go. My father would spray, and a group of reds would go upstairs to Mrs. Pergoli's apartment. Mrs. Pergoli would spray, and the reds would come down again. There was one with a blue spot who came home three times. Imagine my father promising me a trip to the ice-cream parlor the day we found our blue on the kitchen floor with his legs in the air."

They unfolded the blanket and took it to a softer place. It was not so much a seduction, she decided afterward, as a blundering by degrees, from a hesitant holding of hands to the loosening of clothes, until he opened his eyes and asked what *she'd* done, and looked at his watch for advice.

"What is the man doing with you?" Karaghala demanded when she arrived home. He made a loop with thumb and forefinger and pushed another finger through it, questioning her with his eyes.

"For God's sake, Daddy," she said. "Do you mean a wedding ring, or what?"

There was no word from Roger, and Karaghala said it was possible to make a man like that disappear for good. Johanna tried to pretend she didn't hear him. When Roger did call to ask if she'd meet him at the stable again, it was a two-month-old insult.

Roger *had* disappeared, she explained to her father when she hung up the phone. On his own. He'd been an experiment gone wrong. He did phone twice more, calling her his "land-fill heiress." The last time she thought he must have been drunk, because it was after midnight and Roger became abusive, asking what could have possessed him to take up with a woman whose father used to arrange hunting accidents in New York and Pennsylvania.

Karaghala said he had seen long cars moving slowly past the house, cars that could have had Northern plates. He waited through the first winter, watching from upstairs windows as the hunt rode over his land. In the spring he came out to plant his pecan seedlings.

Johanna worked with him on the fences, stretching new wire over his coops without hens. That summer she traded his limousine for a farm truck, helping him forget the web of roads that tied him to New Jersey.

She had a new friend by then, the next visitor to come by. He was Willy, their neighbor across the creek, a pilot for an aerial-photography service, who asked her to country dances in Stilson, and seemed incapable of hiding anything behind his kind blue eyes. She was already very thick with Willy. He buzzed their house in his light plane, breaking laws to show them his face from the air.

First a man who trampled his fields on horseback. Now one who violated his airspace, her father said. Johanna's people attacked on all fronts.

For Karaghala's birthday Johanna baked him a pecan pie and Willy gave him a framed aerial photo of the countryside with their place circled in black at the center. In the middle of the flattened landscape the house made an easy bull's-eye. Using it as a map, Willy named the surrounding farms and estates for them, following with his finger the dirt road they lived on, to secondary macadam, across the east-west corridor to beltway and interstate. Johanna apologized for Karaghala's indifference, and when Willy left she took his present to the attic.

She doubted her father could despise anyone so open, a man with such large hands for affectionate pummelling, and a wide mouth for laughter. But she was careful not to encourage any intimacy under Karaghala's gaze. Willy would walk over anytime, uninvited, knock Georgette around the yard with hearty pats, call his halloos from their doorway, and march onto their deep rugs with muddy boots.

"You come with us," he would coax, when he took Georgette and Johanna for a walk, and Karaghala, not quite pleased to be thought a cohort instead of a chaperon, always declined.

"Be careful" was his blessing on their evenings.

When Roger returned, Johanna heard the hounds first. It was an unseasonably warm November day, too hot to be galloping horses. She came out to watch their approach. The hunt was on a run, coming over the hill behind the house. She saw their leader in his brilliant jacket swerve away from his jump. He cursed, dismounted, and tied a white handkerchief to Karaghala's new strand of wire. Others piled up behind him, their horses rearing and kicking.

In the saddle again, he circled back and took the fence, far behind his hounds. Half his riders followed, coming fast down the field, over the seedlings. Her father was beside her by then, shaking his fist. They could hear the rest of the hunt calling to one another in confusion and disgust, coming around in front, on the road. Johanna was pulling her father toward the house. Georgette, who had risen to bark at the passing hounds, was prostrate again, panting in the heat.

There were riders stopping in the driveway, looking across the yard and yelling at the house, "Anybody home?"

Unable to hold him back, Johanna had come out with her father to face the riders, mostly women. And Roger had emerged from the pack, jockeying to the front. "Whoever's responsible for that dog," he said, "get it out of the sun. Can't you see it needs water?"

Karaghala was moving toward him, but the horse was prancing sideways, and Roger, riding away, called back over his shoulder, "Take care of that bitch, or someone else will." The women, indignant and erect, moved into a trot behind him.

Johanna led her father into the house, fixed him lemonade, and made him lie on his bed with a magazine. A half hour later he had gone into the yard again. Georgette had been untied. She was gone.

Karaghala told Johanna to get her walking shoes on, to change into pants. From her room she could hear him telling himself what a pleasure it was going to be to knock the interfering lover boy off his high horse. She was almost ready when she looked down from her window and saw her father spinning away in the truck.

The hunt had passed over the road, moving away cross-country. Johanna drove south, away from the river, toward the paved highway. A man and woman leading two horses told her yes, they had seen a truck, but they thought the hunt had doubled back to the east. They were looking for it themselves.

She had made almost a complete circle and was approaching their house from the other direction when she heard gunfire and saw hounds coming from the woods into the field above her. She was out of her car, running toward the tree line, when she heard the next reports and saw riders come breakneck into the open, toward her father's fields again. One of them fell forward, wrapping arms and legs around his horse's neck. He regained his seat and galloped past her, yelling, "Gate please!" But there was no gate.

Explosions again, and more riders entered the field and raced past on either side of her. A final shot, and a last horseman bolted out of the woods. Following the rest, he took the jump downhill over the white handkerchief.

Over the next rise Johanna could see down to the creek bed, where her father's truck was parked beside the mill. Closer, she watched him reload a pistol, aim, and fire at six cans set up on a log. Beyond the noise and smoke, like a row of charmed soldiers, the cans were still standing when his gun was empty.

When Johanna and her father got back to the house, there was Willy playing in the yard with Georgette. Johanna brought out three fresh glasses of lemonade to celebrate. Karaghala told why he had hurried off to the mill—for pistol practice. And Johanna told why she had headed for the village—an errand at the drugstore. Halfway there, she said, she'd decided it wasn't important after all. They were lying for each other and for Willy, who told how he had untied Georgette to take her for a walk and then returned to find the place deserted.

Johanna understood Willy only wanted to prove to her father they could all live there happily, the three of them and Georgette, waiting for pecans and grandchildren. But Karaghala wouldn't put the gun away. He was talking about solid wood, something tall that you couldn't see through or jump over, a real privacy fence.

From far off in the hills they could hear the hunting horn, the sound of horse people trespassing. Karaghala raised his pistol to the horizon. "He's a little confused right now," Johanna told Willy. "Not sure what he ought to be shooting at."

They watched him level the pistol again and fire imaginary bullets into the northeast. The horn sounded fainter in the hills. Karaghala looked at Johanna and Willy for a moment, trying to catch the soft things they were saying to one another, before turning back to his missing target. It was as if he was aiming at New Jersey but trying to hit something in Virginia.

"Don't worry," Johanna said. "I think Daddy knows you're going to be my lover."

Willy said he'd never heard of putting a privacy fence around twenty acres.

If a man came along who could build one, Johanna told him, her father might give him anything in his kingdom. She took Willy's hand and carefully led him into the house, assuring him of a safe place inside the fence once he had finished it.

OUR JANICE

Janice Wheatley had heard all these things said about her: Janice is just a wonderful person. A self-made wonder. We are nine times blessed to have Janice. Janice can sew a button on a child's cuff with one hand and stir oatmeal with the other. Who else could get this crowd off to school in the morning? Toys part in front of Janice. She looks you straight in the eye. Our West Virginia au pair.

And she had overheard: Actually Janice gets a little salary. Would you believe the bright thing never finished school? I think she's smarter than some of our own. So much clear-eyed common sense. Our personality gal. The weight problem is under control. I wouldn't say she's plain, really. Her friend Tommy has settled for plumbing. He does some wiring without a license. We don't think he's going to marry her. What's going to happen to Janice when our children are all grown?

In the twelve years Janice had lived with the family, Mrs. Elliot had seldom spoken critically to her. The two of them could chat like sisters, and the children had been advised by both parents that "*pair*" means equal in French. There *was* the problem of the telephone for a while. Too many calls for Janice from Lorraine, with whom she took dance exercise two nights a week.

The littlest children, of course, thought her beautiful, but the older ones were used to catching her in front of the pier glass in the front hall pushing her round face into new shapes, or turning sideways, helping the mirror narrow her girth. They tried to be polite when they corrected what their father called Janice's West Virginia grammar. And she forgave the children their horrid moments. Stephen, at five years old, saying, "I wish you were dead." He cried so pitifully afterward he had to be comforted by Janice herself. Caroline, at nine, asking, "How long are you going to live here, anyway?" That time, Janice retreated to her room behind the kitchen to wait for the apology, which came within the hour: "I hope you stay with us forever."

At the Elliots' there was always a baby coming. As soon as one walked off to pre-school, another was delivered to the nursery and care of Janice. Eventually the older ones returned to her for comfort and advice: How to kiss a girl. How to kick a ball as far as a boy could. How to make someone stop pinching. How to make babies.

Janice Wheatley came to the Elliots from Martinsburg, where her father and three brothers worked as day laborers in peach and apple orchards. At seventeen she hadn't heard of au pair, but her daddy brought her over the mountains to the northern-Virginia Piedmont for an interview anyway. She didn't like leaving her boyfriend, Tommy, a half day away. Even when she lived in the same town with him, he hadn't been steady. There were going to be three children to watch at the Elliots', with a fourth on the way. Janice's daddy predicted there'd be more.

There were nine. "And that's it," Mr. Elliot said, though Janice, who tidied up the master bathroom once a week, had reason to believe Mrs. Elliot was still capable. "They never asked us for more than a baseball team," Mr. Elliot was pleased to tell you. Janice herself would explain to anyone, "My Tommy had his mumps when he was sixteen. If we got married, we might have to adopt."

One thing Mrs. Elliot was careful not to tell anyone was what happened each time Tommy came over to visit from West Virginia. There was a guest room with a lumpy double bed that she knew must keep its occupants awake and aware of one another as they struggled through a night. Appropriate for a love match, out of the question for restful sleep. Before Tommy's frequent visits Mrs. Elliot prepared the room herself, making the bed up with pillows on both sides, setting flowers on the night table. Then she'd lie awake hoping to hear Janice climb the stairs from her room. Afterward, just as anxiously, she'd listen for her descending steps.

The children had no need to concern themselves, and Janice never made enough noise to disturb them. The five oldest slept on the other side of the house anyway. Brad and Billy, called "the boys," though there were five boys in all, had adjoining quarters closest to the guest room. They'd ripped out a threshold board to make a smooth lane for a bowling set and for remote-control tanks they sent into battle from one room to the other. The youngest—Chris, two—and his sister Sally shared the nursery in the same wing with Brad and Billy—the wing with easy access up the back steps from Janice's regular room.

The old log-and-stone house had been remodelled for stylish country living. Mr. Elliot said a Southern general had ridden his horse into the front hall and straight out the back door in pursuit of chicken thieves. Janice could see that such a ride today would require a leap into the yard over two heat pumps outside the back door, which blew warm and cool air, according to season, through fourteen rooms.

Most of the inside walls had been stripped, wired, insulated, and refinished before Mr. Elliot had agreed to buy. All satisfactory work, except in the dining room, where he didn't see why he should have to reach overhead to the chandelier to turn on the light. There should have been a switch on the wall. Tommy always said he was going to fix one for him, no problem, but never seemed to get around to it.

The money came from Mr. Elliot's work in the city at a job he never explained to Janice except to say that he told some companies how to speak to the government. There was always enough for pleasures and doctors, even private schools for the ones who seemed to need it. The whole family took three weeks in Maine every summer.

The Elliots had a long custom station wagon with window space in back for all nine blond heads. Each August, as they climbed up the turnpikes to New England, Janice sat in a rear seat, trying to keep her dark hair tucked under a kerchief and watching other travellers stare at her family. They did make a spectacle sitting down to a meal in a motel restaurant, each of them encouraged to hazard an order. They didn't seem to mind all eyes in the room turned to their table, or when a waitress, overwhelmed, would bring others from the kitchen to witness the size of her task and the cheer and wonder of a resemblance so many times repeated.

Waiting for their food, all of them would play Twenty Questions. The older ones coached the younger, even Chris, who was allowed a turn though he answered "Yes" to all questions, including "Animal, mineral, or vegetable?" When he got bored they helped steady him as he toddled back and forth from Janice's lap to his chocolate milk.

Last Christmas the Elliots' card was a beautiful color photograph of the children ranked by size beside Janice—a stairway of towheads, with Janice's dark hair for the landing at the top. The photo was so clear you could see the colors of all their eyes—brown and green and shades in between. When they showed it to Janice she walked two fingers up the blond steps of the print, naming names, from Chris at the bottom to Patrick at the top, her hand leaping off his head and coming down with a thud on her own. She could always get the children laughing with a simple gesture like that.

On a Friday afternoon in April of Janice's twelfth year in the house, her Tommy arrived after several weeks of not calling. His face was puffy, the way it got, Mrs. Elliot thought, when he'd had too much of the medicine he said was for allergies. Instead of taking Janice to a matinée, he carried in an electrical kit and got right to work on his surprise, which Mrs. Elliot suspected was just a ploy for regaining Janice's good graces after another of his long, unexplained absences, or his way of paying for the room he hoped she'd prepare for the night.

The trouble, he said, was the dining room's log-and-plaster walls. The switch would have to be in the low end of the room's slanted ceiling, where only the parents and older children could reach it. What he'd have to do, he explained to Mrs. Elliot, was to cut through a knee wall up in the guest room and run a wire from the junction box there down to the new station.

"Push it," he told her when he'd finished. "Now turn it." The smaller children were thrilled. "It's a dimmer switch," he explained.

When Mr. Elliot came home they all celebrated with a dinner under the handiwork—meat pie under a full hundred watts and apple crisp in a setting of just a few candlepower.

During the meal Janice's friend Lorraine called. She wanted to know whether in the jazzercise routine done to the words "I want a man with a slow hand" your hips bumped left or right on "hand."

"What's all that about?" Mr. Elliot wondered. And Janice demonstrated for the family, singing along with her performance, her hips rocking close to the table. Someone said, "Gross."

After dinner two of the children stood on chairs to play with the switch, and when Janice held Chris up to brighten the room for himself, he said, "I turned the dark off. Is your friend living here tonight?"

"No, he's not," Janice answered for Tommy.

"Is everything all right, dear?" Mrs. Elliot asked her later in the kitchen. "I was so proud of you tonight." While working at the sink Janice had already overheard Mr. Elliot ask his wife, "What's the point, if the switch has to be in the ceiling anyway?"

For some reason the lights weren't working in Patrick's room upstairs in the other wing. Tommy had left soon after supper but said he'd come back Sunday to fix that, too. Then the lights in the boys' room were on again, off again all through the weekend, and Janice had to keep calling Tommy back with the alternating news.

Monday night Patrick complained that his lights were on but not bright enough for homework. The next evening he charged down the stairs past Janice and into the basement.

"They were blinking on and off," he told her afterward. "I thought someone was playing with the fuse box."

At dinner that night Caroline said she had a riddle she'd heard at school: "What do you call a good-looking woman in West Virginia?" Then she wasn't sure she should finish. But no one was really worried, because Janice had taught them that jokes are like shoes: "Before you bring them in the house, you wipe any dirt off them."

"What *do* you call her?" Mr. Elliot asked.

They were all quiet, waiting to be entertained.

"A tourist," Caroline said.

All of them, the ones who got it and the ones who didn't, turned to Janice. Chris, who knew there was something wrong with a long silence, stood up on the two phone books in his chair and began climbing over laps on his side of the table until he reached her and waited to be hugged.

"Young lady," Mrs. Elliot said to Caroline, "you owe someone an apology," but Janice was already leaving for the kitchen, Chris in her arms.

When the fire came, there was time to go all through the rooms to make sure they were empty. Two of the boys had been playing with the dimmer switch again, ignoring their mother's order to stop. Once everyone knew the switch controlled not just the chandelier but the outlets in Patrick's room upstairs, they had plagued him with blackouts and dimouts and staccato bursts of light and dark. If he quit his room for relief, others would go up to take turns being teased in his place, and the game rang through the house: "They're on! They're off!"

Most of them were in the yard when Mrs. Elliot saw smoke coming from under the eaves. The children had just been given garden chores when their mother screamed, "The house!" Mr. Elliot raced inside to the telephone and the rest of them scattered in and around their home, looking for the fire.

Afterward, Janice recalled that when she yelled at all of them, "Come back from there!" she was holding Chris's hand. Then she had left him in the front yard with Brad and Billy, warning them all to stay right where they were while she and Mrs. Elliot went back inside to clear the house of any others.

Mrs. Elliot said that when she came back out the first time she counted all nine children but Janice was still inside. Then Mr. Elliot came out and told them the fire must be behind the walls upstairs, that it wasn't too bad yet, that he couldn't see flame. He and his wife went in for another look.

When Janice came out the kitchen door she counted only seven in the yard. Caroline, she was told, had taken Sally and gone for the neighbors. Still no sound of fire engines. When the parents came out again, smoke was billowing from the attic vent. Mrs. Elliot was very upset not to be able to see all nine children at once. Her husband said he was going in one more time to make double sure the missing pair hadn't gone back inside. "Don't move," he said. "Don't let anyone out of your sight."

But Mrs. Elliot became frightened, thinking he was too long in the house, and she went in again to find him. Flame came out a front dormer. Some of them ran to see what was happening in back, ignoring Janice, who followed, scolding.

When Mr. Elliot came out he was momentarily blinded and hardly able to speak. The volunteer firemen were telling his wife to lie down until she could breathe normally again. They didn't think they could get inside; they were going to spray through the windows. Janice was counting, trying to make eight become nine.

"She's not making sense," Mrs. Elliot gasped at her husband. "Now she's talking about horses."

Janice was trying to say horses have returned to their stalls in burning barns. When they understood, the family went racing around the yard, while Janice stood right in front and called out, "Chris, I want you to come here right now!"

While their house was being rebuilt, the Elliots turned their disaster into another fable about Janice. Never mind Tommy and his frightful wiring job. "Can you believe *her*? The way she rallied the children and then stood there at the front door, ordering the house to give back Chris?"

"Don't make me out a saint," she told Mrs. Elliot.

They had figured out how Chris had made himself invisible, crouching between the heat pumps at the back. When he heard Janice calling, he had come directly toward her voice, pushing through the back door, where firemen had refused to enter. The wind rushing in behind must have carried him forward, making a tunnel of fresh air for him under the smoke as he moved past the flaming staircase. Moments later the front door blew open and they saw him coming over the threshold, stumbling forward into Janice's arms.

Janice was leaving them, but they didn't believe it. Yes, she said, this time, instead of promising which year it would be, Tommy had said which day in July. But Tommy hadn't shown his face to them since the fire. What she wanted, Janice said, was for the new living room to be the chapel. Her father would come over from Martinsburg with the champagne, to give her away. Lorraine would be maid of honor.

"She's *making* her wedding happen," Mrs. Elliot told her husband. "It's too sad. The boy doesn't even call. He could make her very unhappy."

Janice had told them where they'd all stand during the service and which hymns they'd sing; the children would make a beautiful choir. She was doing her own dress. They had no choice but to get the house ready and have the justice of the peace on hand.

On the wedding morning she was still arranging. Sally, the flower girl, was to walk as slowly as she knew how. No fighting over the bouquet, and Mrs. Elliot's crying was "only confusing the little ones."

"Popcorn instead of rice," Janice said, "because as soon as you throw it, rice disappears." After champagne and cake, when Janice had gone to change into travelling slacks, Tommy lined the escape route through the front hall with children, pouring the popcorn into their hands, telling them, "This is the way you bliss the bride."

WORLD
AFTER DARK

They chose an October day with no wind. The year's accumulation of dry branches and brush was raked into a single pile at the back of the field, and the oldest child, Charlotte, was given the matches. There was a quick blaze, the best part over too soon for the boys, James and Clayton, who went back to tossing a punctured rubber ball into a bushel basket nailed to the old sheep shed.

Because Charlotte got to start the fire, she was chosen to stay and tend the embers. Roma agreed with Abe that they had to give her more responsibility. After all, she was fourteen years old. Where the heat of her young heart was concerned, they were being more careful.

Charlotte had been out at night with a neighbor, Gerald Ray, one of the new-style farm boys with long hair. And she'd come home with puffy lips and corn tassels stuck to her clothes. But Charlotte was good about her fire duty—standing there for more than an hour, though Roma knew her thoughts were away across stone fences. Afterward, Roma let her go up to the house alone to use the telephone. In private, as she'd requested. Her brothers were kept outside, where they could not harass.

That night, after dark, Abe looked out their bedroom window for a last check on the fire and saw a small flame licking at the edge of the ashes. "It can't go anywhere," Roma assured him. "There's nothing left to burn." Already in bed, she lifted the covers for Abe.

"Something's burning," he said.

"I want to talk to you about *Charlotte's* flame."

"But what could be burning?"

"We hardly know Gerald. I don't think he wants us to. He's a bit of a sneak."

"It's not going out," Abe said. "It's moving."

He was dressing again, putting on his boots. Roma was left alone. From the window a few minutes later she could see him stamping on the stubborn fire. There. No, it sprang up again. He put it out a second time, and again it came to life, reminding her of the trick candles they put on the children's birthday cakes. She watched Abe walk without urgency to the shed and return with a spade.

Soon Abe was smacking at the flame, which now was advancing in a narrow line. Roma put on her robe and stayed at the window. It was mystifying but hardly dangerous.

When Abe had worked halfway up the field she began to worry—not so much about the fire as about Abe's exertion. He would beat furiously and the little blaze would die away, then burst up again, moving ahead in a straight path. She called out the window that she was coming to help, dressed, and ran outside, waking the children with her commotion.

"Get another shovel," Abe called.

"Why not water?"

Two more flames sprang up from the first line at right angles, burning in opposite directions, one toward their small barn, the other toward the watering trough on the far side of the field. James and Clayton came stumbling out in their underwear, wanting to help, but were told to stand back with Charlotte, who thought the whole thing was going to be blamed on her.

The fire was getting out of hand. The first line was moving up toward the house, and Roma was going for water whether Abe liked it or not. The kitchen faucet ran very slowly. Plumbing by Abe. And while she waited for the bucket to fill she saw that it was leaking. By the time she got back, there was nothing to pour her water on. Abe had dug a little trench in front of each flame and all fires were out.

On his hands and knees, sniffing the ground, he was wondering aloud if he could have spilled gas along the two lines, maybe from the mower. But he hadn't mowed there for months. The fire had come spontaneously out of the earth through a thin cover of honeysuckle.

Seeing the black scar in the moonlight, Roma whispered, "Someone burned a cross in our field!"

That night she went to bed with a vision of a can of clear liquid, flammable but odorless, sprinkled on their property by a hateful hand. "Do they think we're Jewish, Catholic, octoroons? Is it Abe's name? Abraham? " she asked herself.

Roma had a history of difficult nights. When she was younger she sometimes walked in her sleep. Lately she just talked. One night, according to Abe, she sat up suddenly in bed and said, "Did someone come for the kitchen steps? The kitchen steps. Have they been taken out yet?"

"We do all our own carpentry," Abe reminded her. "Couldn't we discuss it in the morning?"

"No, Abe! You know I have to make this up as I go along."

Abe's laughter brought Roma out of her trance that

night, and she slid back under the covers, awake and without a notion of what had been said.

On the night of the cross she sat up thinking. Her family belonged to no ethnic group or organized religion. They never made a fuss over race. The boys could be horrid and used shocking language but only with each other, and Charlotte was, well, beautiful, a target only of love.

"Do you think it's because we're nothing?" she asked Abe.

"Are you unhappy here?"

"How can you ask?" she said, thinking of the children's secondhand clothes and the peace she had made with slow water in the kitchen and damp spots on the bedroom ceiling that would dry in spring when Abe went up on the roof with a bucket of tar and a broom.

This autumn had been very like the one Roma remembered fifteen years earlier, when she and Abe had arrived in Worton, Virginia, and bought the little cottage with the sloping field behind it. The foliage was brilliant and the crystal air a magnifying glass bringing single trees on the distant mountain into focus. Fifteen years ago she had looked down the lane at a world made for retreat and pleasure. Shining in pregnancy, she was carried by Abe over the threshold of their new home in a village unknown to restoration carpenters and realtors.

They had brought everything they had from their home in Washington in a rental truck—crossing into their new state over Chain Bridge just below the Little Falls of the Potomac. She'd heard the bridge was named for the chain gangs who built it. "Wrong," Abe told her. "It was the chains in the original suspension system." Whatever. She knew Virginia still used prison gangs on the roads. She was coming into a territory, she believed, where criminals had real trouble with the law.

In Abe's loving eyes Roma was a woman "not afraid to use the world after dark." She was going to be a pioneer with him in the new economics, a prosperity that grew from minimal income, no taxes, clever craft, and husbandry. There were young people all over the countryside hiding under the nation's economy. Roma and Abe had come to join this frontier, not as hippies or layabouts but with a vision of a quiet, honorable success.

"Not afraid to use the world after dark." She was proud of that. He meant her former city fearlessness. Muggers be damned, rapists be warned. She would have fought back with tooth, nail, or purse bomb of a blinding spray. She walked to bars on her own, talked to anyone she cared to.

There had been a child coming when she and Abe moved to Worton. That child had been Charlotte. Who now had to be watched. But ever since they'd moved here they'd all been under scrutiny by their neighbors—especially by Mr. Ray, who worked the farm next to them and lived there as a tenant. An unlikely bit of fate that their Charlotte and his Gerald should have matured in the same year. Biological magnets, that's all it amounted to, Roma hoped. That was dangerous enough.

Even in the beginning Mr. Ray never smiled. He'd turned up their very first day, assigning himself to them as a prophet of misfortune. His work shirt, done up to the top button, made a tight noose at his Adam's apple, so that the veins stood out on his neck. His wife, Roma heard, was housebound with emphysema. There was no formal introduction, but words began to pass as if in acknowledgment of proximate habitation.

"It'll cost some plenty keeping all those horses through the winter."

Roma had allowed that it would.

They were opening a riding stable. "Abe's Choice" they'd named it—which meant any of the seven horses in their barn, first come, first served. From the start, Mr. Ray watched the operation with interest, observing the lameness, tardy shoers, eager vets, and customers who misused the horses, galloping on the gravel roads.

The stable had been a clinker. Even Abe admitted his mistake. The local people who could afford horses already owned them. Roma wound up mucking the stalls and packing sandwiches for city cowboys who came for one-day thrills, the same people who might hire a raft to squeeze excitement from the Shenandoah's meagre rapids, or climb the rocks at Great Falls.

After three seasons the horses were sold to a summer camp. By then Roma had a second child, Clayton, and was pregnant with James. She had little time for stable duty anyway. When Abe announced they would grow grapes in their field, it seemed a sensible switch.

Trellises replaced the horses in the pasture. "Don't fight the earth," they were advised. "Find a grape that's comfortable with your soil." They chose the Chardonnay, convenient for sale to the local winery. Abe pruned and tied his vines with a gentle care. Out of season they looked so sere and brittle it was hard to believe they could bear. And then one summer the grapes appeared, a beautiful canopy of pale green.

They had some fine years before a fungus wiped out a whole crop and then killed every vine. "The grape cancer," their man at the winery called it. In the midst of their troubles Roma heard Mr. Ray tell a sombre crowd in the corner store, "Enough drunkenness in the country without help from Worton." Telling this to people who would normally ask Roma how Abe was doing and if the children were over their colds. As though he had a stake in their failure.

"Remember," Abe told her, "we didn't come here to get rich." He imported thirty head of sheep from a neighboring county. They would tend an innocent flock and maintain dominion over their property while they waited for a new five-year plan.

Eventually, Abe announced the new crop would be asparagus. He tore out the failed vines and began to dig long trenches that had to be filled with layers of gravel, sand, and topsoil before he could set in the asparagus crowns. As the shoots came up, he would add more topsoil and fertilizer according to schedule.

To keep the sheep off the asparagus beds, there would have to be paths. This meant fencing the ex-vineyard into quadrants with sheep runs between them. The first run would take the animals from the little barn, where they'd be sheltered at night, to the watering trough on the far side of the field. Another run would go from the pen behind the house, where shearing and dipping would be done, to the adjacent field, a rocky pasture where Mr. Ray's boss had agreed to let them graze for a nominal fee. To hedge their bets and keep their heads above water, Abe started a little classified-advertising sheet, *Abe's Country Trader,* hiring the small press in the village to run off his first copies.

When Clayton and James were small, Roma liked to watch them playing among the flock in the far field like little shepherds, trying to make the lambs their pets. But as the boys grew they had no use for the animals.

Of Mary's little lamb, James believed the words to the rhyme were "its fleas was white as snow," and Roma saw that their own sheep and the boy's country grammar school were doing nothing to relieve his confusion. The sheep moved along the paths Abe made for them, not wagging tails but spilling pellets. Grass processors they were, getting themselves jammed up in the lanes between the fences, bleating, their backsides hopelessly matted.

Abe went after the wool himself. In shearing, you had to be quick, nervy, turning the animal over between your legs, immobilizing it while you moved with resolve. Two sheep bled from seven wounds, and a third escaped, its fleece hanging half off its belly. With the children screaming at him to stop, Abe gave up.

No one wanted the sheep slaughtered. Unruly pets with no purpose in the scheme of marginal survival, they were attractive to neighborhood dogs, who chased them into the crossed lanes between the fences, where they cried for help, trapped in gridlock with only one intersection.

For two summers Abe let all the asparagus grow into willowy ferns. In the third spring, with the roots fully established, he began to cut for market.

In the good asparagus years they sold as many as two thousand bunches to supermarkets, vegetable stands, and city restaurants. Even James was eventually trusted with an asparagus knife. The whole family worked on hands and knees, harvesting the shoots. A warning, passed from Mr. Ray to Gerald to Charlotte, that "the little boy could cut his finger off" was ignored, along with his advice to get their house some lightning rods.

They had always used rock salt for weeds, but what to use for the tiny sticklike insects, iridescent red-and-black beauties, that appeared one summer in the asparagus ferns? A lingering poison would be a crime against the land, Roma said. Instead, she prepared an organic spray of garlic and water. The asparagus beetles took wing. Abe danced a jig with Roma up and down the rows. To think they were showing farming could be a gentle art instead of a deadly science.

Their success was on display for all who passed by. In the early evenings they could see Mr. Ray, on his way to the store, interrupting his walk to stare at their field. "Whatever he wants to tell us," Roma said, "he can't bring himself to come through the gate." She suggested Abe wait beside the road for him and give him an easy meeting to get to the bottom of this.

But what should they do with the sheep? When the animals were not trapped in the fenced paths between the asparagus beds, they were liable to stray through fallen sections of stone wall into the road. Two lambs disappeared, and Roma sent the children to search up and down the road and ask at each house in the village. Everywhere the answer was the same. If they weren't drowned in one of the ponds, the dogs must have got them.

In the end it was Mr. Ray who assumed the duty of sheep cop. One day Roma saw him lift a matted ewe over the wall and drop her roughly on her own side, as if the animal were aware of its trespass.

"We have to sell them," Abe said when she told him what she'd seen.

They couldn't find a single buyer for the whole lot. And the awful bleating as the sheep were herded into a truck for the auction yard let Roma know whole families were being betrayed. Abe was busy tearing down the fencing.

Roma's words woke Abe that night. "When you let the lambs go, you have to expect a row from the ewes."

"Roma," he said, "we let them all go."

"I know. But there was enough grass. The table is set for everyone, isn't it?"

"Roma, wake up!"

It wasn't Abe but Roma who sat on the wall a few days later, waiting to meet with Mr. Ray. She caught him by surprise, and he raised his hand to tip a hat that was not there. "Fine," he said, startled.

"How are you, Mr. Ray?" she asked.

He was avoiding her face, looking beyond her, toward the asparagus. "You want to be careful," he said. "The beetles aren't the half of it." He seemed so tired, probably worn down by his hard life on the farm, and so much grayer than when Roma had first seen him, fifteen years earlier.

"About the children . . ." she said.

"We can't be responsible for what comes over our fences at night, can we?" He gave the issue a contemptuous toss of his hand, and with that he was on his way again.

Back in the house, Roma took Charlotte into her room and shut the door. "What do you talk to Gerald about? Where do you meet him?" Charlotte was face down on the bed. Roma began rubbing her back. "If he's going to see you, sweetie, he ought to come to our door."

"He's afraid of his father."

For the two weeks of the month Abe travelled the county promoting his suddenly successful *Country Trader*, Roma sat by the phone taking ads, ignoring activity in the field. At the end of the second week she learned what Mr. Ray had meant about the asparagus. First there were the black specks the beetles had left cemented to the ferns, then the slimy larvae, and the plants eaten down to brown skeletons. All while her back had been turned.

After the damage was done, Roma spotted Mr. Ray in the road again, nodding as he went past, agreeing with himself, as if this had been the only just end to it all. Odd, she thought, that the son should go unseen except by Charlotte, while the father was almost daily in view, passing with his slow gait and calculating gaze.

With the sheep fencing down and the asparagus dead, the land went rapidly back to wild seed. There was orchard grass, the honeysuckle, some clumps of wild rose, and locust shoots. Something new for Mr. Ray to cluck at—a neglected field.

One evening that September, the kitchen faucet stopped running altogether. Abe and Roma went out to check the well with a flashlight, and there at the bottom in several feet of water were the carcasses of the two missing lambs. Abe went down with ropes to lift them out. The lambs might have fallen in and drowned. Roma couldn't be sure.

Across the field she saw the silhouette of a great skeletal hand moving in the breeze. As she walked toward it to prove to herself it was only the limb and branches of an old apple tree, Roma saw two figures slip away from her in the darkness. She ran back, calling, "Abe! Is Charlotte with you?" and her daughter came out of the house to ask what in the world was the matter with her.

Charlotte had created a new game, Fiction Pictures, played with the family's aging Polaroid. All summer she had staged unlikely events and documented them on film. One, titled "Little Big Man," showed James, not five feet tall, slam-dunking his ball. Actually he was jumping down toward the basket from a platform of cinder blocks. Another, called "Long Way Down," had Clayton falling from a second-story window, his scaffolding hidden from view.

As long as they remain fiction pictures we're safe, Roma thought. But that was before the two lambs, before she began to look for eyes in the village that might be more than un-friendly. That fall the children were especially quarrelsome. Clayton was getting into fights at school. He told Gerald, who was big enough to thrash him, to stay away from his sister, and gave Charlotte bruises on her arm to prove he meant it.

"Stand up for your sister," Roma warned him.

"That's what I am doing," he said.

Charlotte made faces but gave Clayton a wide berth. James, frightened that Gerald might really hurt his brother, stood in the doorway crying out his alarm if he saw Clayton or Charlotte sneaking out after dark.

On the night of the cross, Roma was surprised and grateful to find that the children were all home. When the fire was out and they were all back in their beds, she went to each of them and said there was nothing to be afraid of. And then, back in her own bed, she asked Abe, "Do you think it's because we're nothing?"

Roma didn't believe Mr. Ray had done it. But she could imagine him nearby in the night, approving. "By his lights," Abe said, "we're dogs in the manger. If we don't know how to use the land, we ought to get off it."

In the light of day things looked no better. Mr. Ray told the clerk at the store that the cross was just the old sheep business. When his words were repeated to Roma they sounded disparaging but mysterious. And ominous. Abe didn't think they should bring the police into it. The culprits would be named in the fullness of time. Easy enough for Abe to say. But for Roma time was already too full, with her children morose and resentful, confined to the house after sunset. She tore to shreds Charlotte's latest fiction picture, a shot of James, goggle-eyed, flat on the floor, with ketchup coming from the corner of his mouth.

Why did Mr. Ray go so slowly past their place? What right did he have to linger that way, passing judgment? She went out to meet him again in the road, and he tried to walk around her.

"There's nothing to talk about," he said. "If you'd just keep your girl home."

"We had a cross burned on our field."

"It was the sheep," he said.

Was this some sort of country shorthand? Were they paying for some perversion he'd witnessed, something to do with the animals?

After the fire Roma had difficulty sleeping at all. She'd wake and leave Abe alone in their bed while she felt her way through the dark house, checking doors and standing at their window. "You can't stay awake every night watching for prowlers," Abe told her. Surprisingly, things were going quite well—maybe too well—with his *Country Trader*, which was selling handsomely. Roma was afraid Abe might not follow through on his success.

"I don't see anything wrong with a taxable income, do you? It wouldn't be immoral or debasing, would it?" she asked, as if their practice of marginal subsistence lay behind their troubles in the community.

"It wasn't part of the plan," Abe said. But he thought they could tidy up around the house, maybe paint the trim and keep the grass shorter in the front yard. A signal to Roma that it would be all right to go through the family bureaus, discard some of the older things, spend something on clothes for once. Nothing virtuous in being down at heel. It could even lead to bad posture, turned ankles.

That year Roma had suddenly noticed how many farms in the countryside around them were breaking up, the land being cut into convenient shapes whose underlying symmetry was economic. There was horse fencing everywhere, and ten-acre horse people. Not a society for their family to join, though it wouldn't be wrong to get a pony for James, who wanted to ride Western, with boots and a lariat. Why should he have to throw an imitation basketball at a make-believe iron hoop for the rest of his childhood?

The night Charlotte broke away, escaped after curfew, going out over the porch roof with the help of wisteria vines and the promise of James' silence, Roma was downstairs in the parlor with Abe. She was saying, "We can afford more. Even the children can see the hypocrisy. It's obvious to the neighbors, too."

Abe had come up with a spiritual theory to explain the cross. "What these people see in us," he said, "is people who have no moral core, outsiders who profane the land with silly projects."

"They, they, they!" she said. "We're looking for a *he*. At most a couple of them."

James came down from his bed in his pajamas. Trembling with split allegiance, he informed on his sister, who had already been gone for an hour. Roma ran up to her daughter's room, and called down to Abe that it was true. "Clayton's gone, too!" she said. "I'm calling the Rays."

"What could they tell you?" Abe asked her. "Charlotte won't be there. You'll only make trouble for Gerald."

But Roma was looking for the number. Abe couldn't take the phone away from her. She was dialling.

"This is Charlotte's mother," she said.

There was labored breathing at the other end of the line, probably the sound of Mrs. Ray's emphysema.

"Is Charlotte there?" Roma asked.

She couldn't get Mrs. Ray to speak to her.

"Is Gerald there?"

There was silence, and then Mr. Ray's voice on the phone. "Is this the girl's mother?"

"Yes."

"Don't worry about Gerald," he said. "We'll take care of Gerald." Then he hung up.

Roma was just making plans for a search, dividing up the neighborhood with Abe, when Clayton came back.

"Where have you been?" Roma asked. "Where is your sister?"

"Out there in the fields somewhere. Where she always goes."

Before they could set out after Charlotte, she was back, too. She didn't try sneaking in her window but barged through the front door without apology and sat down beside Roma. With her coat still on, she told Roma she had broken off with Gerald. "All he ever wanted was something at night. Like I wasn't supposed to hang around him in daylight."

One fine November morning, standing in his pasture where only the faintest traces remained of the fire, Abe saw that Mr. Ray had been right all along. A cross had been formed by the two narrow aisles that ran between the field's former fences, the paths where the sheep had gone single file between the asparagus beds. Their droppings, ground into the earth by their hooves, had set an organic fuse waiting to be lit by the bonfire.

"Nitrates!" Abe said, delighted with a solution that pardoned all his neighbors.

For the children, that season Roma bought new coats, shiny red and green, all filled with something Abe swore was as good as goose down and cheaper. And they painted every room in the house with an off-brand of latex he found on sale. Cosmetics now, Roma said, quality later. To reshoe the family might cause a few blisters in the break-in period, but this time new leather for everyone.

Mr. Ray's shuffling vigils did not let up. After fifteen years, he was still curious. If we're poor, why don't we work, Roma said. Maybe he wonders if he could get by without a real job, too. After all, it's his life that's in danger when the farms are sold.

Abe said she was talking herself into a solidarity with Mr. Ray and all the other farmers in the neighborhood who might be wondering what would happen next in her tricky field.

But Roma was easy again walking out at night in the country lanes, comfortable with the whisperings and shadows of farm boys and their sweethearts dropping out of sight behind the fencerows. She let Charlotte take a moonlit picture of her in which she appeared ghostly in the semidark, floating over the road behind their wall, though her feet were on solid rock.

IN DAIRYLAND

"So why don't you leave?" Kate asked.

"I am leaving," Louis said, and promised he wouldn't be back for anything in his room. They could do as they pleased with his things.

Kate and Christo watched their son walk down the gravel drive to the public highway, the only way off their place without trespassing on Dairyland. "He won't go far hitchhiking with a shotgun and bedroll," Kate said. Then she was up the steps, two at a time, to check his room.

"It's gone," she called down to her husband. "He must have taken it with him." The diary Kate was looking for, the one Louis kept faithfully, the one she read regularly, usually sat on the boy's bureau. The thing was, he frequently left it propped open to his latest entry. She was sure he intended them to read it, and just as certain they were not meant to acknowledge they had.

There were times it had been difficult for Kate to remember what she was expected to know and what she was supposed to pretend she didn't. For instance, what *should* she have said about her son's new interest in Jennine Lenoir, the daughter of Tenant House Number Two at Dairyland, the huge farm that surrounded them? In his journal Louis had described her as "a really nice girl who needs someone to show her the way off the farm. She doesn't need the lipstick."

Christo thought if Kate was going to call the girl "different," she should have been ready to explain to Louis just what she meant. "Admit it," he said. "You've been taking potshots at him for weeks. You pushed him right out the door."

"We love him enough to let him go" was all Kate could think to say.

For years Louis had been a friend of underdogs and a leader of small movements. As a senior in high school, he befriended the boy who wouldn't pledge allegiance. And he made passive resistance work for a gym class that sat in front of lockers for forty-five minutes refusing to move for an abusive instructor. This year, in his job at the sawmill, he told a driver making less than minimum wage it was against the law for him to take the company truck across state lines. Closer to home, he tried to defend the farmer who was fired for poaching on Dairyland, which had always been posted against hunters.

Kate had to admit she wasn't quite comfortable with Louis' crusades. If he was going to continue to move and shake, it wouldn't be behind her apron. For an hour or more after Louis walked out, she stayed on the phone letting closest family know just what had happened. "He called us names," she told her sister. "Me a bitch and his father an ass." For her mother, she explained, "At seventeen it isn't running away, it's just leaving home."

"He's free as one of your Canada geese now," Christo said, after she'd run out of relatives to talk to, but Christo said he doubted Louis would try migration. It was already November, with frosts every night in their Virginia countryside. Deer season had opened, and high-powered rifles echoed all day through the darkening hills.

"Can we leave the geese out of it?" Kate asked Christo. "Just for once."

"He might try to shoot one," Christo said, reminded of Louis' diary entry in defense of the fired tenant: "His family is hungry. Why shouldn't he kill his game where he finds it?"

Kate doubted her son would shoot into her flock. But how, she wondered, were people going to tell him apart from any weirdo wandering in the hills with a shotgun? Before going to bed she went again to check the outside thermometer. It was holding steady at twenty-eight degrees.

It had always been accepted in Kate's family that she brought the Canada geese to Dairyland through a wishful and ingenious husbandry. It all began when she and Christo still took long walks through the woods and fields of the farm's three thousand acres, before their relations with the big dairy had soured. Kate had seen the first gander and his mate nesting at the edge of the farm's great pond a dozen years ago. And the same season she had watched in dismay as a fox carried the gander away.

What the geese needed, she'd said, were floating islands as sanctuaries. The next year she had carried several inflated inner tubes to the pond. With twigs and brush she made nests in their centers and then anchored them on the water with rope and bricks. If the geese nested successfully, they would always return.

Christo had said it wouldn't work, that snapping turtles would pull the goslings under as easily as a fox could snatch them from the banks. But another gander arrived with his mate, and from time to time the two of them could be seen riding on one of the rubber islands. Louis, then six, used to follow his mother over the meadows when she went to spy on the new family's progress.

Year after year the geese had returned, and the flock had increased wonderfully, until there were nearly two hundred of them. Kate said their leader was the same goose that first nested successfully, the one that led their V in the sky on all trips to neighboring cornfields and on their annual Canadian flights. She could identify this bull goose, she was sure.

If she knew anything about it, Christo told her, she'd know the flock switched leaders now and then. He doubted she could tell one from another anyway. In the evenings Kate would watch the geese pass over their house, but she no longer saw them make their beautiful landings on the great pond. The field walks had ended when the new owner came and converted the farm into a model experimental dairy, hiring Mr. Oberkreutz as manager.

Oberkreutz has been rude to all trespassers, even neighbors. As soon as he arrived he surrounded Christo's house with heavy American wire fencing and ran it down both sides of their driveway. After that, Kate and Christo saved their sympathies and fence chatter for the several tenant families, the dairy hands.

The evening Louis left, Kate watched her son thrust his chin forward as he passed down that narrow strip of land that was their only easement to the world at large. She suspected his anger might subside before he reached the far border of Dairyland.

Louis had gone only a half mile down the road when he climbed through the fence onto the big farm. He was heading for the huge pond but keeping to the creek bed, the lowest contour of the land, out of sight of the manager, Oberkreutz. Through the bushes he could see Jennine's father, Mr. Lenoir, on a tractor far across the landscape, preparing ground for some new miracle seed. He felt sorry for Mr. Lenoir, whose leg had been broken twice, kicked by cows. Sometimes his sons walked behind him imitating his limp.

Lenoir had been here when the place was an old-fashioned dairy. He used to squirt milk at Louis' socks when the boy hung around the barn for evening milking. But Lenoir's sons had been given the new, strange chores. They were the ones who had to learn to hook the cows up to the plumbing and switch on the electric fingers.

Louis dropped his bedroll, pointed his gun at the line of geese swinging low in front of him, and did not shoot but found himself aiming at a square of green blocked out against the bank. Coming forward, he was amazed to see that someone had built a lean-to between two trees, right beside the water. The roof had been framed with thin pine poles, and woven into the poles were double layers of green boughs. Whoever built it had known just what he was doing. The back faced the northwest weather, and the open front looked up the hill in the direction of the farm buildings. He'd have had plenty of time to see someone coming. The floor was a soft cushion of pine needles, convenient for Louis.

Kate was busy letting more people know what happened. Christo could hear her on the phone telling someone, "The thing is, we still buy most of his clothes and ask that he try a little harder to take care of them. Some of them are stuffed with down and quite expensive. It's like this. A jacket is new. It's torn at his job at the mill. He patches it with duct tape to keep the stuffing in. In a few months, when it's half silver with the tape, it's easier for him to forget where he took it off. Then the recriminations."

Afterward, she asked Christo, "Why am I telling them that? Silly of me, blaming it on clothes." What she was afraid of, she said, was Louis' being a target for a deer hunter, or that someone on the big farm would mistake him for a poacher. That evening, for the first time in months, Kate climbed the fence into Dairyland. She was headed for the milking barn.

Ahead there was the clanking of stanchions, the stomping of impatient hooves on the concrete floor. There were no prize bulls on Dairyland, only hundreds of extraordinary mothers whose daily gifts were measured in extra gallons. The farm was a center for bovine engineering; all semen was imported, all insemination artificial. Kate could imagine the experiments continuing until there was no more room for an udder between cow and ground.

Inside, the milking machines were on. Air bubbles and the white fluid were moving through clear plastic tubes. Printed in large gothic capitals over doors at either end of the barn were signs that said "TREAT A COW LIKE A LADY" and "THERE'S NO SUCH THING AS A CONTENTED COW."

"We are busy here. Can I help you?" The voice came from behind Kate, startling her. Oberkreutz was moving between two rows of cows, coming toward her.

Kate explained about Louis, and Oberkreutz called one of his men over. "This is Mr. Lenoir's boy Dwayne," he said. "He's not very smart, but he will help you look."

"I don't want to look for Louis," Kate told him. "I'm not even sure he's around here. I just wanted someone to know he might be." It occurred to Kate she had betrayed her son, but when she saw Mr. Lenoir outside the barn she told him, too, thinking someone friendly ought to have the same news.

"He's not gone far," Lenoir said. "My girl, Jennine, saw him on the road this morning and gave him a ride to work."

Kate knew Jennine had been putting herself in Louis' way a lot more than she used to, standing around the barns where she could be seen from their house. Jennine was supposed to go away to one of the state colleges this fall, but her family asked her to wait a year. A happy girl, she twisted her mouth when she laughed as if she were blowing out a candle to the side of her. Tall and supple, she could toss a bale to the third tier on the hay wagon.

Jennine had been on a family errand to the village when she passed Louis on the highway and offered him her off-balance smile, but didn't stop. Then, seeing him in her rear-view mirror waving his arms, she had turned back. "What's the gun for?" she wanted to know.

"I'm not staying home anymore," Louis told her. "I just keep it with me all the time. In case there's a rabid coon or something gets in my way."

Jennine took him to his job at the sawmill, and on the way Louis asked if she'd like to visit his campfire. She said she'd pick him up after work if she could get the car again. And bring sandwiches or something. She watched as he absent-mindedly pulled bits of down from a hole in his jacket sleeve. With each feather removed, another popped up to take its place. Jennine laughed and told him it was like a box of Kleenex, but when she let him out of the car she said, "Your people let you dress common, don't they?"

On a clear, windless night, his second night at the pond, Louis killed one of the Canada geese as they came gliding overhead, preparing to land on the water. The bird fell into the pond several hundred yards away, and the flock wheeled off in another direction. There was no way to eat his goose. He couldn't even retrieve it.

How many times had his mother told him, "In Dairyland, geese are the real sacred cows." A flight of geese, he remembered her saying, is a serious thing. There are no frivolous or sharp turns. Long journeys are point to point, all trips at controlled altitudes. Like members of a show squadron, they're at pains to maintain equal separations.

I'm separating one for good, Louis had thought, blowing his goose from the flight pattern, hoping the sound of his gun had been muffled by the noise of distant farm machinery. A few moments later, hearing an engine, he ran into the woods. It was Oberkreutz, coming his way in the pickup truck, right toward the pond, as fast as he could get gates open and closed behind him. He raced along the shore, then came toward the tree line. From fifty yards deep in the forest, Louis could see him looking through his windshield into the trees.

"Go on," he said, "get going," watching Oberkreutz head back toward the barns, probably going to tell everyone that a poacher had been shooting at his geese, that the birds weren't on the pond. Coming out of the woods, Louis could see his goose still floating on its side.

In the morning the bird was gone. Louis wondered if it was a stray or had always been one of the Dairyland flock. According to his mother, the first bull goose came deflected by shotguns at the Chesapeake Bay. She thought it must have been one of the thousands that winter over on the Eastern Shore, feeding in the wide cornfields on the harvesting machines' mistakes.

"Your goose was lost," Christo told her.

Geese don't get lost, she maintained.

Louis, grateful he wasn't listening to talk about geese,

shook the pine needles from his clothes and blankets and headed for the highway, where Jennine was waiting in the car.

"Look at you," she said, sliding over to let him drive. "You need a bath."

"Where were you last night?" Louis wanted to know.

"I couldn't come," she said. "Maybe this afternoon."

When she told him they thought he shot at the geese, he admitted it.

"But they're almost tame," she said.

"They're wild Canada geese," he snapped back at her. "They don't belong to anyone. To Oberkreutz, or my mother, or anyone."

That afternoon, when the saws were quiet for a moment and the rest of the crew at the mill was gabbing in the company shack, Louis slipped away from work with Jennine. He had the sweet smell of fresh-cut poplar on him, and as she came closer on the car seat to sniff his neck she said, "Louis and his little tenant woman."

With no response for this piece of truth, he just drove a little slower. "You know," he finally said, "your family doesn't have to take all that stuff from Oberkreutz. I bet there's a lot of other places they could work."

Back by Dairyland, Jennine showed him a wagon path where they could hide the car, and the two of them went hand in hand toward the big pond. "Where did that come from?" Jennine asked, approaching the lean-to.

"I thought you might know," Louis said. "It was just here."

He walked a few steps up the bank, then turned to explain, "They were coming right over my head. This is where I was standing."

"Big boy hunter," Jennine said, coming up beside him.

There was still a lot of daylight left and not much cover, even in the lean-to, but on their way into the shelter she was already helping him with the buttons of his shirt.

Sliding next to him, she felt something under her. "What's this?" she said, pulling a notebook from beneath the blankets.

"Something I write in," he said. "About things that happen to me."

"Am I in it?" she wanted to know.

"I guess you'll have to be now," he said.

Christo had left work early, too, called home by Kate for a noon treat of wine and cheese. She was hoping he'd say wise and moderate things that would leave them both reassured about Louis' future. Instead, the special luncheon had turned sour. Kate, going on about her flock again, said she'd heard that one of them could distinguish between three types of hybrid field corn.

"You know what I'm sick of?" Christo said. "I'm sick of magic geese." He wouldn't stop. "You know what I mean. The lone goose mourning his dead mate, or the deserted goose waiting through sad seasons for the unfaithful lover. The stuff about mystery radar leading them south through the dark November nights."

"Enough," Kate said.

"Look, all you have to know about geese is they have a memory. Don't pretend they're superhuman. They *can* get lost. But if you flew that high you could follow the coastal outline without asking applause for navigational skills. There's some disorder in the lives of all species," he said, calming.

"What about ants?" Kate asked. "What about bees?"

The cheese was finished without further mention of

geese. But when they were through, Kate turned to Christo and demanded, "What else?"

"Put a little romance in your own life," he advised. "Flap your own wings a little. The way Louis is."

Someone at the mill who knew the Lenoirs had called their home to say Jennine came for the boy in their car well before quitting time. He just wanted to make sure the family knew what was going on "since Jennine isn't really that grownup yet."

When Kate saw Mrs. Lenoir coming over the fence she could guess why. "If you see my girl, could you tell her she's wanted at home?" Mrs. Lenoir said, unable to raise her eyes.

"It was so sad," Kate told Christo afterward. "The way she stood there apologizing for bothering us. As if she were degrading the doorway. She wouldn't come in. Jennine is such a bright light in her family. She's so worried. They could be out there in the fields somewhere."

"Well," Christo said. "She's a nice girl, isn't she?"

"What's the matter with you? It would be just awful if they did something that couldn't be undone. Mr. Lenoir would be so hurt."

"You're presuming a lot," Christo said.

"Yes," Kate agreed, "and we're going out to look for them. Before they do something stupid. Like stay out all night together."

Christo and Kate, hunting across Dairyland, saw Oberkreutz on the hill in front of them, looking down toward the pond. A moment later they saw Mrs. Lenoir come from another direction. When Oberkreutz turned and saw them all he waved them back and walked quickly toward them. Mrs. Lenoir veered toward them, too, and then they were all standing together, Oberkreutz doing the talking.

"Ah, it's terrible. They are not there again. I think they have been scared good. Perhaps they will no longer come here. We can't have this."

Kate was thinking, How can the man be so obtuse, when Christo turned to her and said softly, "He means the geese."

"Ya, what did you think?" Oberkreutz asked abruptly. "Now, can I help you? What did you want here?"

"We were just walking," Christo said.

"But this is not a park," Oberkreutz told them. Dismissing Kate and Christo from his view, he turned on Mrs. Lenoir. "Where are your boys? No one is at the barn? It is so late already for milking."

Oberkreutz set off for the distant barns with great strides, and Kate was trying to keep up with Mrs. Lenoir, who didn't seem to want company. "I'm sure they're being sensible," Kate called ahead to her. "If they're together, I mean."

Louis came home again, but with plans for taking an apartment in the village. He'd thrown away his diary, or was keeping it out of sight, though he told them he'd be seeing Jennine when he felt like it. Kate wasn't concerned. She knew the Lenoirs were keeping a tight rein on their daughter, that she had to be home before dark. She was pleased to think that Louis and Jennine had only been involved in the way of a pleasant friendship. She had heard the girl tell her son, "You don't dress much better since you ran away from home," surely a sign of a healthy distance between them.

With Louis' departure for his village apartment, Kate told Christo how proud she was that her son had behaved so well through all this, and of the way he kept a cool, sensible head on his shoulders. It was all right with her if he wanted to keep the little details of his outdoor adventure to himself.

"He shot one of your geese," Christo said.

Kate turned on him. "How do you know?"

"And if you really want to know, he made it with the girl. Right there by the pond."

"You read this?"

"I didn't need a diary," Christo said. "Louis told me. He's not the least bit ashamed of it."

"You mean they were out there when we came looking? Oberkreutz might have seen them?"

Christo thought the couple had probably seen Oberkreutz coming and moved their party into the woods.

In his diminished family Christo had less concern for rules, more time for contemplation. In defiance of Oberkreutz he'd been walking out in the evenings over the Dairyland fields. And, for the first time, he'd taken an interest in the geese, watching the flock glide down for its nightly landing on the pond.

After a couple of weeks of his trespassing Christo said he had to show Kate something; she had to come with him on his evening walk. She said she'd join him but only after Christo agreed to a circular route around the fields so they wouldn't be seen from the farmhouses. Kate couldn't bear to be caught out there again.

She and Christo were on the hill, looking down at the lean-to, when the long line came honking over the trees. The birds were shifting from V to straight line to V, and then a second line was visible coming along the ridge and falling in behind the first formation. They passed overhead, and Christo whispered, "Watch this."

Over the center of the pond there was an abrupt change

in their flight. The whole skyful of them broke ranks. They tumbled left and right, all honking at once. There were midair collisions and mayhem as they hit the water, flapping wildly. It was as if there had been a flock decision for cannonballs and belly flops, for utter disorder. "They've done it three nights in a row," Christo said.

On the way back to the house, Kate was looking for explanations. "They must do that when they're supremely happy," she said. Still struggling against claims for natural disorder. "They know it's going to be crystal clear, with a full moon. They'll be feeding all night long. The combines are finished. They can see the cornfields speckled with yellow— But how did he stay warm?" she interrupted herself.

Christo had examined the lean-to several times and had tried to describe it for Kate. Simplicity itself, but built with loving care, the boughs woven so neatly through the framework. It might even be watertight. Still, he couldn't imagine who would have built it, whether it was some hunter who wanted a regular place to shelter from the dew, or if it was just there for idyllic seclusion, for someone who might want a quiet place to berth for a season.

To Christo it had been no more extraordinary than the overnight appearance of a mushroom on the lawn. But for Kate there was no excuse for a structure whose intention was so clearly fugitive. No one on the farm had built it, Oberkreutz assured them. An attractive nuisance, Kate called it. A complaint with a legal echo that must have chafed the German. When Christo went for another look, it was gone from the face of the earth.

A NOTE ON THE TYPE

This book was set in Fournier, a type face named for
Pierre Simon Fournier, a celebrated type designer in eighteenth-
century France. Fournier's type is considered transitional in that
it drew its inspiration from the old style yet was ingeniously
innovational, providing for an elegant yet legible appearance.
For some time after his death in 1768, Fournier was remembered primarily
as the author of a famous manual of typography and as a pioneer of the
point system. However, in 1925, his reputation was enhanced when The
Monotype Corporation of London revived Fournier's roman and italic.

Composed by Graphic Composition, Inc.,
Athens, Georgia
Printed and bound by The Haddon Craftsmen,
Scranton, Pennsylvania

Designed by George J. McKeon